Saving Turtles

Short Stories

by

Jim Pahz

These stories are works of fiction. Any similarity of the characters to people living or dead is coincidental and unintentional.

Stone Cottage Press
2020 S. Mission, Suite 232
Mount Pleasant, Michigan

Cover illustration by Robin Shipman.

ISBN - 10 0-9824158-4-2
ISBN - 13 978-0-9824158-4-9

Dedication

This collection is dedicated to
my three grandsons,

Kevin, Erik and Josh

who keep me laughing and
fill my life with adventure.

Table of Contents

*Co-authored with Cheryl Pahz. The Secret, Easter Surprise and Bad Hair Day, are excerpted for the novel **Almost Chosen...Nearly Saved**. Paradise is excerpted from **Quetzal,** and The Favor comes from **McAngel**.

LUCKY

Monday morning, six a.m. I open my eyes just as a giant hand scoops me up and hurls me across the room where I smash into the wall. Only it isn't the wall, it's the floor. And the giant hand, I don't know what that was.

Perspiring profusely, I begin to throw up. The room is spinning. My wife and daughter scrape me off the floor and somehow manage to get me into the car. All I remember hearing is, "Emergency room. Drive faster."

Arriving at the hospital I am triaged. Six new nipples are glued to my chest. I am wired to a machine, I assume to be an electro cardiogram.

"Squeeze my fingers," the nurse demands. Another says, "Follow my finger with your eyes."

"He's clammy, diaphoretic."

* * *

Given medication I'm wheeled to my room.

A while later another man is wheeled in. He is my roommate. The nurse asks him how tall he is. He answers he is six feet tall. It isn't true. He is no taller than I and I am 5'6". The man is thin and has a Fu Manchu mustache that hangs over his lip. He says his name is Melvin.

I introduce myself. "Do people call you Mel?"

"No," he says, "they call me Melvin."

"Okay. I hope you feel better soon, Melvin."

"I came in an ambulance," he replies. "Chest pains. I'm lucky to be alive."

"I'm glad you made it."

"Yeah… me too."

Later a doctor comes to tell Melvin all his tests are negative. The doctor says he doesn't think Melvin had a heart attack.

"Is everything okay at home?" the doctor asks.

"Not really. I have a lot of stress. There's tension, if you know what I mean. Sometimes I feel like I might explode."

"Sounds like anxiety. Are you on something?"

"For depression," he answers, "Paxil, and Zoloft."

"I see," the doctor says. "We'll talk some more

tomorrow. Rest now."

After the doctor leaves, Melvin starts telling me his story.

"My marriage failed. I used to work as a truck driver—long distance hauling. One day, after I had left home, the dispatcher called me and said I wouldn't be working until the next day. I turned my truck around and went home. When I arrived I found my best friend in bed with my wife. I confronted her and told her I loved her, she said she didn't care. She loved my friend more than me. That's what she told me. Those words cut like a knife. My two sons are grown now, but they won't have anything to do with me. I haven't seen them in years. You see, my wife poisoned their minds against me."

"I'm sorry," I say. "It must be difficult for you."

"Yes," he replies, "it is, but I have a fiancé now. We have been living together for three years. She says she wants to get married, but I don't know. I'm not sure. Her two older girls say they hate me. It makes it hard to live in a family where people don't like you. There's a lot of stress. There are three younger children who still live at home. The eight-year-old is hyperactive and, well, he's not fond of me either."

"I'm sorry."

"It's hard, but I keep birds."

"What?"

"Birds. I have chickens and some guinea fowl, and a few ducks. I had pheasants in the past and sometimes turkeys. The pheasants flew off."

"I see."

"I think I'm happiest when I'm around my birds. Sometimes I think animals are nicer than people. Do you know what I mean?"

"I think I do."

"I called my fiancé and asked her to come visit me, but she says she can't. I called her three times. She always says she's too busy. She keeps giving me excuses. I hope she picks me up when it comes time to get out of here because I came by ambulance and I don't have a ride home."

*   *   *

When my doctor returns to give me my results he

says I didn't have a heart attack or stroke. I'm lucky.

"You have an infection in your inner ear," he says. "Behind the ear drums your ears are filled with fluid. It's referred to as labyrinthitis. You have lost your equilibrium and that's why you fell over. It's also why you threw up. Basically, you are seasick. I've put you on steroids which should lessen the inflammation. I gave you an anti-dizziness medication also. It will help stop the vomiting, but it will make you sleepy. You're going to have to wait until the fluid drains and your brain fixes itself. I want you to remain in bed a few days and under no condition should you drive a car."

I stay in bed and slowly the symptoms subside. The following afternoon Melvin's fiancé comes to get him. She is an exceptionally attractive woman—not thin or fat, but in perfect proportions with a long free-flowing mane of blond hair. She wears heavy makeup and a tight fitting skirt and high heels. The fabric of her skirt is shiny, as if it was made from plastic or leather. I thought this woman could be employed as an anchor on a cable news network. She is that good looking.

She walks right by my bed scarcely giving me a glance.

"This is my roommate," Melvin says.

She looks in my direction and nods her head. She doesn't smile. Then she turns back to her fiancé.

"I'm going downstairs to the lobby," she says. "I need to find the man who will wheel you in the wheelchair. They don't want you to walk by yourself. Probably has something to do with liability."

After she leaves, I say. "I don't know what I was expecting, but it wasn't that. Haven't you ever heard the song about marrying an ugly woman—if you want to be happy? I mean, especially considering what you told me of your first marriage."

Melvin laughs. It's the first time I have seen him smile since meeting him. "Other people have told me that," he says. "She's a real looker, isn't she? She's hot."

"She's very pretty," I respond.

"What can I say?" Melvin sits up straight and puffs out his chest—like one of his chickens. He is bursting with pride.

"I'm a lucky man," he says.

A few minutes later the attendant arrives to wheel Melvin to the lobby.

Jim Pahz

THE FLOATING CITY

My story starts with the interrogation of a prisoner. It happened a long time ago during the holy wars in the East. We thought the captive was a Muslim, but he insisted he wasn't. He said he was Christian from New Eden, the floating city.

I laughed at him and said, "Sure you are. New Eden is a legend. It doesn't really exist. Nice story, but the place isn't real."

"It exists," he replied without inflection to his voice.

"Then why don't I know anyone who ever came from there?"

"I came from there," he replied. "I guess you know me. You see me sitting here in front of you. You're not blind."

"Well," I responded, "I don't exactly know you now, do I? Besides, I don't see the Cain mark anywhere on you." I looked more carefully at his hands. I was always told when a person wears the Cain, it is on the palm of the right hand. The mark is said to look like a little dagger.

"I don't have the Cain," the man said, opening his hands. "Only invaders are marked with the Cain. There is no reason why I should be marked. I was a citizen, not an invader. I left when I was fifteen. On my own, you understand. Nobody forced me to go. Not a smart thing to do—leave, I mean. But I did it. I don't have anybody to blame but myself."

I looked down at the man and almost believed him. He was convincing. *What the hell,* I thought. *I might as well play along.*

"Okay," I said. "Suppose you tell me about New Eden. What's it like there?"

"What is it like?" he repeated. "It's perfect. It is the only place I've ever been that has absolute harmony. Everyone is comfortable. There is work for all. Nobody goes hungry, and nobody dies from the plague. I never saw a person die from any disease. Sure, people pass away, but they are old. It's their time."

"I don't understand," I said. "If this place is so

wonderful, why did you leave? Why would anyone leave? You weren't driven out like Adam and Eve, I presume?"

"I don't know the answer to that question, and I've asked myself hundreds of times. I was just fifteen when I left. I was bored. Maybe that's what people die from there, boredom. I wanted to see the world and have adventures, to fight and go to war. I wanted glory and to do the things I thought a man does, besides farming or watching sheep. I don't even know why you'd need to watch sheep—there aren't any wolves there. Probably the only place in the world without a wolf. It's hard to explain, but when you have everything you need and you're fifteen, you feel like something is missing."

At that moment, I felt pity for the man. Wherever he was from, it was obvious he was unhappy and quite delusional.

"It sounds like you left paradise. Why don't you just go back?" I asked.

The man looked up at me and smiled. "You don't think I've tried? I'm thirty-three years old. I've been trying to get back since I was seventeen. I almost made it, too. It took me less than a year to realize what a terrible place this world really is. But, the city's not there now."

"What do you mean it's not there?"

"It floated away. That's why it's called the floating city."

"What do you mean?"

"I mean, it floated away, like a feather in the wind. It went someplace else, and I don't know where. It's always going somewhere else."

"You can't be serious."

"Yes, I am, because I almost made it back. I had to disguise myself because when I got close to the city it was under siege. I thought it was hopeless and the city would fall, so like a coward I fled. Then the miracle happened."

"What miracle?"

"It's like this. New Eden is a Christian city. The chief religious office is run by a bishop named Prester John. He's a direct descendant of Balthazar. A monk told me this, before I left. He revealed the secret to me. The monk said Balthazar was one of the three wise men spoken of in the book of Matthew. Everyone in New Eden practices the Christian faith. It's a holy city like Jerusalem. I was only fifteen when I left and was never a religious person. I thought religion was nonsense and my parents were crazy to believe any of it.

"So I left and wandered for two years. When I was seventeen I decided to return. When I got close to New Eden I found the city besieged by Arabs. The Muslims had already overthrown the Christian king in Jerusalem and were now turning their attention to New Eden. The city was completely surrounded, and it seemed only a matter of time before it would fall. At least that's what I thought. Those within had defeated other invaders, but that was in ancient times. They had the practice then of branding their enemies with the Cain mark and afterward refusing them entrance to the city. But now the Muslims were so numerous it seemed impossible to prevail against such an army. When I looked at the city it was like a corpse covered by millions of ants.

"I learned that inside the city, the governing council considered all options—the people could surrender and beg for mercy. They could convert, or they could commit suicide like the people of Masada had done so as not to be captured by the Romans. The council was at a loss to know what to do. Finally, Prester John asked for three days of prayer and fasting before any action be taken. He told the council he would beseech God, Himself, to intercede. He said that was the only hope for the people of New Eden.

"All the people gathered and prayed. They prayed and fasted and on the third day the miracle happened. There was a terrible noise. Thunder clapped and lighting flashed from the heavens. A rift in the earth was torn with great trembling of the ground. I watched the city, and the ground it rested on, lift right into the sky above. It hovered there for awhile and then floated away. I saw it pass with my own eyes while I remained hidden from the invaders. Where it settled, I can't say. But I believe it went somewhere further east. Now every Easter the city rises as did our Savior. Then it floats away and lands somewhere else. It's a truly miraculous place."

There wasn't any strategic information we could get from this prisoner so we decided to let him go. I didn't know what would become of him, and I didn't care. I thought the man mad or perhaps possessed. Cities don't float. Everybody knows that, and his story was beyond belief. We left him in the wilderness weeping for his lost paradise and cursing the world around him.

I forgot about this man for many years, but to be truthful, I never completely forgot about New Eden.

* * *

After my stint in the army I returned west to my homeland. A marriage had been arranged, and I was paired with a woman named Elizabeth. I worked hard, and soon my wife and I had two boys. We named them Joshua and Erik. During the days I worked in a grist mill using the power of the river to grind wheat into flour. It was hard work, twelve to fourteen hours a day. At night to relax I'd stop at the tavern to drink. But I always returned home to be with my family. I worked in this manner for about ten years and saw my boys grow tall as reeds before my eyes. I believe I was happy then, but I was tired and there was never enough of the things I wanted.

One evening, I sat in the tavern at a long table. I watched a woman applying powder to the window sills.

"What are you doing?" I asked.

"Fly agaric," she answered. "You know, the mushroom powder."

"Why?"

"Too many flies. The powder makes them stupefied."

"What?"

"Stupid. They can't think right and get confused. Then they're helpless—easy pickens."

I looked at the windowsill and noticed several flies buzzing around, going in circles, apparently unable to fly. Then the woman came along and swatted them with a piece of straw matting. She looked up and smiled a broad toothy smile, except she was missing a front tooth.

"Got 'em," she said. "Sometimes I mix honey with the powder. Then they get stuck real good. They die a slow but sweet death. I like that." She spat on her hands and wiped them on her apron.

"I see." I said, repulsed by the woman. I took a long draw of my ale and looked in the other direction to avoid further conversation with the fly killer. That's when I noticed a man at the other end of the table. He was a coarse-looking fellow with dark hairy arms and a full beard. He was sitting alone, and as he drank I watched the ale run down his beard and drip on the table. When he let go of the mug and turned his hand over, I saw the mark on the inside of his right palm. It looked like a dagger.

Curious, I moved myself across from him and offered to buy him a drink. I could see he appreciated the gesture. When I was certain he was favorably disposed, I spoke.

"That is an interesting mark on your palm," I said. "Is it self-made?"

"Not hardly," he answered. "Acquired that when I was East—the floating city. They branded me like a steer. I'm trying to get back now. We're raising an army to defend Prester John, the Bishop of New Eden."

"You mean there really is such a place? You have been there?"

"Of course I have. We were taken into the city and treated nicely, even though we were prisoners. I mean, except for the branding. That wasn't pleasant. But I guess it was worth it; a small price to pay. I saw all manner of things in that city I wouldn't have believed."

I interrupted the bearded man and asked. "I once heard that there were no wolves in New Eden. Is that true?"

"I couldn't say," the bearded man replied, "I didn't see any, but I did see a unicorn."

"Truly?"

"Yes, a sprightly thing it was, with an ivory horn in the middle of its head. There were all manner of creatures in New Eden. I saw giraffes and griffins and strange-looking birds as big as a man. But I don't recall seeing no wolves. And the gold and jewels—you can't imagine such wealth—indescribable. But the most remarkable thing was the well right in the heart of the community. It's the well of perpetual youth. When people drink the water from that well, they never age. That, my friend, is the real attraction."

"And you left such a place?"

"I had to. No choice. I was an invader. I was lucky I got out with my life. You see, I wear the Cain." He opened his hand revealing the black dagger print on his palm. "But I tell you this. Had I stayed, and if they had let me live, I would be ten years younger today. I figure if I return to help fight against the infidels they might let me stay. If not I will kill Prester John and stay anyway. Perhaps you would have a mind to ride with us?"

*   *   *

I would indeed!

I was immediately overcome with thoughts of New Eden and the treasures that awaited. It's as if the desire had been in me for the past ten years, simmering beneath the surface. Now it boiled over. When I told Elizabeth, she didn't understand, and she did her best to dissuade me.

"You have everything you need right here," she said, "a family, a house, and a good trade. Your boys love you. We have been blessed. We have what all people want. If you leave, what will become of us? Think of your sons. How will we live? You will jeopardize everything."

"Quiet, woman," I said. "This is what you call happiness? I am aging. I work from dawn until evening, and you think this is all I want in life? There is more. Imagine a world with no disease, where no one suffers or grows old. All the treasure one would want just waiting for the taking, and you can enjoy it forever."

"Nonsense—it's is a foolish dream from a drunken old soldier—a legend at best. If there is any treasure, which I doubt, you can be certain it will be guarded. This is a fool's errand if you ask me."

*   *   *

But I wasn't asking. So after ten years of family life I left home and kin to follow a dream. I headed east and helped the bearded man recruit an army to accompany us. These were rough men and not pilgrims. We told them of the riches we would have and the earthly delights waiting behind the walls. We spoke of the animals, the gold, and of the water that would enable us to live forever. We promised them paradise on earth and said they would live like kings.

The men were excited. "Are we off to the Crusade?"

some asked. "Will we fight for the kingdom of God?"

"No," I answered. "We don't fight for God, we fight for us. We fight to get rich. Let fools die for Jerusalem. We answer the call of Prestor John, and when he lets us in his city we are going to steal his treasure."

They all laughed.

*   *   *

It was a long and arduous journey. Frequently we passed forces returning from the Crusades—small bands of defeated soldiers. They assumed we were going as replacements to fight for God. These men were tired and worn atop horses that stumbled along with heads hung low to the ground. They told us many had perished along the way.

When we reached Jerusalem, we gave a wide berth to the city and headed north and then east. We always tried to avoid people, especially the Knights Templer who were suspicious of everyone. All we talked about among ourselves was the gold and treasure which would soon be ours. Prestor John was the key, even though we planned to kill him.

When we got closer we invaded a small village but found the occupants surprisingly cooperative. They gave us food and made no attempt to be hostile. They admired us and confirmed our plans. They told us if we marched ten kilometers due east we would get to the mouth of a huge gorge. They showed us people who looked little more than children but who claimed they were hundreds of years old. These people had come from New Eden and this was the proof we were looking for.

We thanked these people by not killing them and left their village intact. We went forth like ravenous dogs beside ourselves with greed. The following day we reached the mouth of the gorge just as the villagers had described it to us. We began our march. As we rode further and further, the canyon walls rose higher and the canyon itself narrowed. After about thirty minutes it was impossible to hold the horses back. They were so fired up their nostrils flared and their necks bent against their chest as they looked to the ground. They foamed with lather as we rode—an unstoppable wall of force and terror.

Then I noticed men on the cliffs above. At first I didn't realize what was happening. I saw one or two men—then a dozen, then hundreds. Suddenly we had to pull the horses to a stop to keep them from crashing into the walls. Everything seemed to disintegrate and we lost sense of any formation. It was chaotic.

Looking up at the men on the cliffs, I saw they were holding their hands in the air with their palms open. All I saw were palms that seemed to each have a smudge in the center. When I caught a glimpse of a face or two, it was invariably smiling or laughing. For a moment I thought these warriors were saluting us because we were a superior force. They were admiring and giving us praise. Then I realized they weren't honoring us in any way. They were mocking, and their smiles were grins of amusement.

At that moment I knew what was happening. Like others who had come to fight in this part of the world, I too had come. But I was not motivated by God or to see a heavenly kingdom established on earth. I had come for profit. I had left my family and my good life because I wanted more. I wanted to drink from the fountain and be rich. It didn't matter whom I killed to get what I wanted.

So, on a spring morning in the year of our Lord 1192 I rode into a box canyon looking for paradise. But this canyon wasn't the paradise I hoped to find; it was a fool's paradise. Elizabeth had been right and I was as stupefied as a fly on a window sill.

As these thoughts coalesced in my mind, I saw the sky grow dark and then rain began to fall. But once again I was wrong. It wasn't rain, it only looked like rain. There were arrows falling down—lots and lots of arrows.

THE SECRET*

When I was twelve years old my parents brought home a dog we named Buddy. He was my pal for the first forty-eight hours until I noticed how badly Buddy smelled. We gave him a bath but it didn't help. So I thanked my parents for Buddy and then told them: "No thank you." I lost interest in Buddy and wouldn't let him into my bedroom. I thought my parents would return Buddy from wherever he came from, but they didn't.

That was the summer my parents decided to send my brother and me to camp. I don't know what their reason was but I assume they had the best interests of their children at heart.

My parents sent us to a camp in the Adirondacks. At twelve years of age I wasn't exactly camp material. I was a frail, tow-headed boy who liked being alone and playing with imaginary friends. I enjoyed playing by myself in a make-believe world of pirates or cowboys. I was different from my brother, Mikey, who, although younger than I, was a born athlete. I hated sports and preferred fishing, or drawing, or collecting stamps, or just about any non-competitive activity.

The camp my parents chose was Camp Thunder Bay, on beautiful Raquette Lake. It was advertised as an athletic camp and promised to help kids build character. Every day, weather permitting, the campers were expected to participate in team sports. My athletic inabilities soon became apparent at camp, and I was either teased or ignored by most of my fellow campers. I tried to be invisible. Sometimes it worked, but most of the time it didn't. Nobody wanted to pick me as a team member for any athletic event. Whenever I missed a hit or didn't catch the ball, others would snicker.

"You are the worst," they would say. "The worst softball player, the worst basketball player, you're terrible… you can't do anything. Maybe you can fish," they would say. And I could; I was, in fact, quite a good fisherman.

Sometimes they called me "chicken arm" because I couldn't throw a ball straight. "You throw like a girl," they would say, "a sissy." They also called me "sneaky" because I was never around when I was supposed to be — I was being invisible.

The taunts were painful, but I had no choice but to endure them. When I could sneak away from camp I would wander through the forest. Most of the time I walked alone, but occasionally other boys who also didn't exemplify the attributes the camp admired would accompany me.

Nelson Peters was one such boy. The other campers called him "Mad Dog" but I had no idea why. Maybe it was because he physically resembled a bulldog. He was a bow-legged, stocky-built kid with a flattop haircut and a hair-trigger temper. Frequently he started fights with campers bigger than he. I guess he was trying to prove something. Sometimes he got the crap beat out of him, but he usually held his own and he never backed down. Whatever the reason, everybody kept a respectful distance from Mad Dog. One day Nelson confided to me that he had a secret, which he kept in a blue trunk at the foot of his bed. He was waiting for the right occasion, but promised he would share the secret when the time was right.

Another camp acquaintance was Bruce Lipschultz. Bruce was a small boy with freckles and red hair. Because of his small size and lack of interest in athletics some campers referred to him as Brucie Baby. He wore thick-rimmed glasses and always seemed to be the last, or second-to-last (depending on whether I was present) person picked for any activity. Bruce was a loner and even though the other boys said he was a loser and a pussy, he didn't seem to mind. He always had his face in a book and was oblivious to what the others thought or said of him. When I asked him why he didn't mind when other boys berated him, Bruce answered: "Consider the source." At twelve years of age, I wasn't sure what that meant, but I nodded affirmatively.

Both of these boys, like me, were camp misfits. We weren't about to have our names inscribed on the deerskin that hung on the wall in the social hall. Other campers said of us: "When one of these guys is on your team you might as well be baking a cake." I never understood what they meant by this, but realized early in camp life, that I would have preferred baking a cake than playing basketball.

My two acquaintances and I occasionally came together for companionship or just to complain about camp. But most of the time each of us remained apart from one another—loners. In our own way we endured the indignities of camp life. We were kids and there seemed little we could do about it.

One day when the three of us were together, Nelson asked if we would like to accompany him on safari. I didn't know what Nelson meant until he revealed the secret he kept in his blue trunk: an army surplus rifle hidden beneath his carefully folded pants and tee-shirts. Nelson had bought it with a coupon he'd cut from the inside cover of a comic book. He also had two bullets, each about three inches long, and even at twelve years of age I could easily imagine the damage they could do.

"Camp Thunder Bay is part of Adirondack National Park," objected Bruce. "Hunting is prohibited."

Mad Dog just smiled in his devious mad-dog way and we agreed to accompany him on his safari.

"It will be an adventure." I said.

With a little luck and planning, it wasn't difficult to sneak away after lunch, when the campers were expected to remain in their bunks and rest for an hour. Luckily, my counselor was away from the cabin. The other two boys also managed to escape and were waiting for me behind the wash house.

We hurried away from camp into the forest. Nelson, carrying his rifle, took the lead. Bruce and I followed behind, talking. Suddenly Nelson stopped. He turned his head and put his finger to his mouth, indicating we should be quiet. Then he pointed straight ahead where a deer stood in our path about twenty yards in front of us. The deer stood motionless looking directly at us. We froze. Nobody spoke a word. Nelson slowly lifted his gun and fired. The deer went down, but it wasn't dead. It thrashed about, pawing at the ground as it struggled to regain its footing.

"Holy shit," exclaimed Bruce.

Nelson threw the gun on the ground, then ran directly past the deer and into the forest.

Surprised, Bruce and I looked at each other and then turned to Nelson who had changed direction and ran back toward us, wide-eyed and hysterical, his hands shaking.

"What am I going to do? Oh, boy. Shit! What will I to do?"

The deer was still thrashing, its motions became progressively slower and more erratic. Nelson turned again and ran back into the woods, all the while talking to himself.

I felt my heart pound, but resisted the impulse to bolt. To be honest, Nelson's bizarre behavior fascinated me, I wanted to see what he would do next.

Finally Bruce said in a calm voice: "We should put it out of its misery."

"What do you mean?" I asked, brought back to reality by Bruce's words.

"It's dying. We should shoot it in the head or something. We can't just leave it to suffer."

Nelson came back, still shaking. Tears were running down his cheeks and he was muttering unintelligibly.

"Nelson," snapped Bruce. "Calm down. Get yourself under control. Do you have the other bullet?"

Nelson stopped mumbling and reached into his shirt pocket, but his hand trembled so badly that he dropped the bullet on the ground. Bruce picked up the bullet and put it into the rifle. Walking to where the deer lay, he pointed the weapon and fired directly at the deer's head. The animal gave a jerk and lay still. Bruce lowered the gun and turned to me and said: "We'd better hide the evidence. Get some branches and cover the carcass."

That was a strange word to use, *carcass.* Why didn't he just say cover the deer or cover the body? I was beginning to panic. Again, I wanted to run, but deferred to the authority in Bruce's voice, recognizing him as a leader. Who would have guessed? Nelson, in contrast, was acting like a squirrel in the highway, running back and forth, mumbling to himself and trying to decide whether to go right or left.

"Don't tell anyone," Nelson stammered desperately, still crying. "You won't tell, will you?"

"We won't tell," answered Bruce. Then, turning to

me, "will we?"

I shook my head "no."

"We could get in a lot of trouble for this," Nelson threatened. "We could go to jail. We could *all* go to prison. Swear you won't tell."

"I swear," I said. "I won't tell anyone."

"Me, too," Bruce answered. "Now, help us find some brush and cover the deer."

When we had concealed the body as well as we could, we walked back to camp in silence. At the edge of the forest, Nelson hid the gun under some brush by a large Sugar Maple. We reached camp in time for the next activity without attracting attention. Once again we went our separate ways.

I felt terrible about that incident. For the next few nights, I could hardly sleep. My guilt added to my general distaste for camp life. I had already been feeling sorry for myself, knowing how the other campers regarded me and wishing I could just go home. It was humiliating to be the last one picked for every activity except fishing. Of course, nobody was ever picked for fishing. Worse, I knew the insults were true. I was not an athlete, nor did I want to be one. I'd never asked to come to camp. I wasn't consulted when my parents reached their decision. I assumed my parents loved me, but after coming to camp, I wasn't sure.

Suddenly I missed everything about my life at home, including my dog. I'd hardly given Buddy a second thought, except to complain that he made the house smell. Buddy was a stinky dog. That's just the way it was, but now, away at camp, I couldn't stand to be parted from him. It no longer mattered how Buddy smelled. He was my dog and my best friend.

A couple of days after the deer incident, I lay in bed, feeling miserable and waiting for the bugler to blow reveille. The other boys in the cabin were sleeping, but I couldn't sleep. I felt badly about leaving my dog behind, and felt sure Buddy was as lonely as I was. And then too, there was this business about murdering the deer. I was an accomplice. How long could I keep the crime a secret? I was ready to confess. Would I really go to jail as Nelson had suggested?

That's when I had my epiphany, my moment of

insight. I would leave camp. How simple. What an obvious conclusion to reach. I would just go home.

I climbed out of bed, got dressed, and crept out of my cabin. Going to another building I entered stealthily and tiptoed to the bunk where my younger brother Mikey was sleeping. He was four years younger than I. I awoke him and explained we needed to go home.

"I had a dream," I said, "about Buddy. In my dream Buddy told me to come home. I know Buddy misses you too. I think we should obey the dog. Come with me, Mikey. We can run away together."

Mikey was only eight years old and he loved camp. He excelled at sports and he didn't miss Buddy at all. I thought I would be able to persuade Mikey, but I was wrong.

"Go away," he said. "Get out or I'll call the counselor."

"What about Buddy?" I asked.

"Fuck Buddy."

"What?"

I panicked. Mikey didn't understand the gravity of

the situation. I doubted whether he ever would. That was when I finally bolted and ran from the cabin, straight into the Adirondack forest. I had no backpack or any supplies whatsoever. My only thought was to leave camp, to flee this terrible place and return home to my family and my lonely dog. I might have made it, too, except the camp was on an island. With nowhere really to go, I wandered aimlessly through the woods. Round and round until exhausted and tearful, a search party discovered me covered in scrapes and bruises. I was led back in shame to second activity period—basketball. I hated that sport the most. Even so, I vowed I would not betray Nelson or Bruce. I would never let the world know of the crime the three of us had committed.

I kept my vow until the end of the season. My two acquaintances and I never spoke of the incident again, not to each other or to anyone else. When the summer ended my brother and I came home and only then did I confess my participation in the crime. I told Buddy. He was a sensitive dog and I believed he would understand. Sure, he was stinky, but he was my best friend and he could keep a secret.

WAITING FOR WITNESSES

"You're drifting."

"What?"

"Drifting—driving recklessly. Keep your eyes on the road."

"There's nothing wrong with my driving. I've been driving a long time. And, by the way, I haven't had any accidents."

"Not yet," Charlene said. "But if you're not careful, you will. It's only a matter of time."

"Yes, dear."

The next morning Charlene asked me to help her with a stuck barn door. It was frozen in the ice. I tried to force it open, but all I succeeded at doing was getting her to scold me.

"Watch it," she said. "You're going to break the door. Step back. Move away. I'll do it myself." She gave a push and the door dislodged.

I tried to walk away.

"Where are you going?" Charlene yelled.

"To the house. I'm going to put on a pot of coffee. It seems like I'm just in the way here. Besides, today is Saturday and the Witnesses may come."

"Oh, sweet Jesus, not again."

Once each month, as regular as the appearance of a full moon, the Witnesses came to our house to visit. Carrying their Bible and a few issues of their magazine, the *Watch Tower*, the men would ring the doorbell and stand patiently on the stoop while their women waited in the car. The gentlemen were dressed in suit and tie. That's how you knew who they were. Nobody else would dress so well on a Saturday morning. We lived in the country and were too remote to attract sales people.

Seeing the Witnesses come up the driveway always annoyed Charlene.

"What do those people want?" she asked. "Why are they here—again."

"They just want to talk," I answered. "They're nice

people. You ought to try talking with them."

"I don't have time to talk. I'm busy and those folks always show up at the most inconvenient times. Haven't you noticed?"

Of course, it wouldn't have mattered when they showed up. My wife would have always been too engaged in some activity. She was, in fact, a busy woman, and there was never enough time in the day to accomplish all she wanted to do. The last thing she desired was to stop her important work and sit and gab with strangers.

Myself, I liked the Witnesses and enjoyed their visits. I tried to anticipate when they would be coming next so I could have a pot of coffee ready. The Witnesses were nice company.

"They just want to convert you," Charlene said. "They want you to join their cult."

"It's not a cult. Jehovah's Witness is a legitimate religion, like Baptists, Methodists or Presbyterians. And I don't think they are trying to convert us."

"Then what do they want? Are they selling

something?"

"I think they are selling God. The concept, that is. These are spiritual people, and they believe they have a mandate to go forth and spread God's word."

"If they're so spiritual they should join a 12-step program and leave us in peace. Why do they have to interfere in other people's lives? You know," Charlene said, "I bet they get a lot of doors slammed in their face."

"Maybe so," I answered, "but not mine."

"What I can't understand," she continued, "is what you get out of it. Why do you indulge them?"

"I'm not sure," I said, "but when I learn, I promise you'll be the first to know."

* * *

The Witnesses didn't show up that Saturday, and I confess I was disappointed. Later that morning I decided I would cook some beans. Now, I know beans are an under-appreciated legume, but not by me. Beans are a highly digestible source of protein and if prepared correctly can be very flavorful. I like Great Northern Beans. I add an onion, about a spoonful of sugar and a nice piece of meat. I let the beans simmer for hours. And that morning I let them simmer too long. The water evaporated. I was in the living room watching television when I smelled the beans burning.

"Oh no," I screamed. "My beans!"

"Is that what stinks?" Charlene asked. Then, "You'd better see about your stinky beans."

When Charlene got to the kitchen I was filling the pot with water. I thought I would boil the water to soften the residue of the burnt beans.

"Give me the pot," Charlene demanded.

"I'm washing it," I said. "It needs to be cleaned."

"I know, but you can't do it. What do you know about washing pots? I'm the housewife," Charlene said. "I know about cleaning."

"I'm not a moron," I said. "Even I can clean a pot."

"No, I don't think so. Give me the pot."

I didn't want to give it to her, but I did.

*   *   *

On Wednesday, Charlene and I had a confrontation.

"You look dumpy," she said.

"No I don't. I'm fine."

"No, you're not. You're dumpy. Not firing on all cylinders, if you know what I mean."

"I know what you mean. But honestly I'm fine. I have a little stomachache, that's all."

"See, I knew it. You're not manic like you were the last two days. I suspect you're bipolar."

"Cheese Louise. I have a stomachache. I'm not bipolar and I'm not dumpy."

"It's *jeeze* Louise… not *cheese* Louise. I rest my case. You're on a down cycle."

*   *   *

By Friday she was still insisting I was dumpy. I tried to avoid her as much as possible. It made life easier.

Then Saturday morning, while eating breakfast, Charlene confiscated half of my portion of potatoes.

"What are you doing?"

"I'm taking away some potatoes."

"Why?"

"Because you're putting on weight," she said. "Too many potatoes, Buster."

"But I love potatoes for breakfast."

"I know. That's why you're getting fat. You've got to trust me on this. It's your health I'm thinking of. I'm only looking out for your welfare. Can you understand that?"

"I suppose." And I could. I appreciated that Charlene, my wife and companion, would have my best interest at heart. Besides, I could eat the rest of my potatoes for lunch. It gave me something to look forward to. But an hour later I saw something that shocked and dismayed me. Charlene was taking my potatoes and mixing them with the dog food.

"What are you doing?" I inquired, alarmed.

"I'm feeding the dog."

"But those are my potatoes."

"Well, yes, they were, but not any more. Besides, potatoes are cheap. You can buy more potatoes."

"That's not the point. They are my potatoes—not the dog's."

But, it was too late. The potatoes were gone. She

had already mixed them with the dog food and an egg. They were on the floor in front of me in a stainless steel dog bowl. My spirits sank. At that instant, I was dumpy.

Then I remembered it was Saturday. In an hour or so the Witnesses might come. I thought maybe I'd put on a fresh pot of coffee, just in case. As I thought about the Witnesses I had an epiphany, just like the people in the Bible. It was a moment of insight. I was coming to terms with who I was and what made me tick. I didn't understand all the reasons for enjoying the visits by the Witnesses. Maybe it had something to do with my religious angst or perhaps it was something as simple as I liked hearing myself talk. But at this moment, in this time and place, I recognized one reason out of many. I liked being visited by the Witnesses because my wife, Charlene, didn't.

SAVING TURTLES

Charlie and Linda had been married for two years and were students at Michigan State University. They had driven from Lansing to Traverse City to spend the weekend with Linda's parents. It was a special occasion, a night honoring the twenty-ninth wedding anniversary of Linda's parents, Lester and Martha. The idea was for the family to go out to dinner to celebrate, but it hadn't turned out as planned. Now, sitting in the living room of the Hilyard's house, everybody watched Lester crawl across the living room floor to face his fish tank.

Lester had been drinking for the better part of the evening. He was so inebriated that Charlie wondered whether his father-in-law would need help getting up. Lester lifted his beer can as if to toast the fish and took a long swallow. He put the can down on the floor and turned to the family.

"Do you know how many turtles I've saved? I can't tell you exactly how many," Lester continued, "dozens, maybe hundreds. Whenever I see a turtle on the road, I stop the car and pick it up. That way," he paused for emphasis, "it won't get squashed." Another pause. "I've rescued so many turtles."

"Good for you," Charlie said. He wondered if Lester was too drunk to notice the sarcasm in his tone. Then he added, "I'm sure the turtles appreciate it."

Tonight, Lester's abdomen appeared so swollen it looked like it might explode. *He looks pregnant,* thought Charlie.

Lester turned to him contemptuously. "And what would you know? Have you ever stood in someone else's shoes, college boy? Wait until you get out into the real world." Lester took another drink. He was still on his hands and knees. As he lifted the can high to drink the remainder of his beer, some of the liquid ran down his chin and onto his t-shirt. Some spilled onto the carpet. When he finished drinking, he released a prodigious belch. He smiled and said, "I like these fish." His speech was garbled, and it sounded like he had a mouth full of cookies. "They're honest. They don't keep you waiting. It's something, the way they look back at you."

Turtles, fish, what else? Charlie turned his attention to his mustache, which was interfering with his breathing. He began to curl the ends while Linda sat motionless. She and her mother seldom spoke when Lester was drinking. There would be time to talk later, after he passed out.

In the background, on television, a man was selling knives. Nobody was watching the show. Charlie heard, "…it has a unique type of jigging. The handle is Cancun Blue and is bone. "

Charlie wondered why he and Linda didn't just leave. Last night, Lester had forgotten his anniversary dinner and failed to appear. Only Martha, Linda, and Charlie were there, and they waited an excessively long time in hopes that Lester would eventually come, but he never showed. Finally they went to dinner without him. In the morning, when Lester finally did appear he was full of excuses. But no one confronted him. Lester had done this sort of thing before. It wasn't anything new.

Tonight they pretended nothing unusual had happened the night before. Martha said Lester would feel bad if they mentioned his failure the previous evening. "I don't want to upset him," Martha said. "It might make him feel bad."

So here we are again, Charlie thought. *Another evening in the Hilyard household. Lester is drunk and we sit around and watch him act like a jerk and nobody says anything.*

The knife show played in the background. Charlie remembered he had once asked, "Why is he always watching a show about knives?"

"I don't know," Linda had answered. "It's his favorite show... especially when he's drinking."

"But why? Does he collect knives?"

"No."

"Then why does he watch a show about knives? It's the most boring program I ever saw."

"Not to a knife lover."

"But you said he didn't care about knives." Charlie found the conversation frustrating.

"I said he didn't collect knives," Linda responded. "He might be a secret knife lover. I can't say for certain."

That conversation had been a while ago. Charlie looked at the television. The announcer was talking about razors and said: "It's a good looking piece. The blades are engraved on both sides. This razor is the old style, like Granddad's." Charlie remembered his grandfather had a metal Gillette razor, nothing like the ones being shown on the television show. Charlie wondered how long his father-in-law could keep drinking before losing consciousness. Charlie wanted to change the channel. *I wish he would pass out, then maybe we could watch something interesting or at least we could go to bed.*

Lester mumbled something unintelligible. Charlie thought he heard, "Salt pork… codfish. My own ragged claw… I did the best I could. But, okay… Hey, it's all good. Daddy loves you." Then Lester laughed out loud.

They stared at Lester. Martha said, "Yes, dear. Of course you can."

Can what? Charlie wondered. *She isn't making any*

more sense than her husband.

Lester didn't drink all the time, only in evenings and on weekends. During the week day he was a real estate broker. He worked for a company named *Home Sweet Home* and supervised several salespeople. Lester must have loved his job because when he was sober it was the only thing he ever talked about. He spoke of home sales and how his agency sold more homes than all his competitors. "I was the youngest man in Michigan to ever get into the Million Dollar Club," he said. "And now that I am the boss, my agency is number one—first in sales. It doesn't matter if it's a strong or weak market, we're the best." Lester said the agency needed him because he was a *closer* and a *born leader*. He described himself as a "people person." But Charlie wondered how Lester managed to run an agency at all. *How can he function at work when he is either drunk or hung over?*

When sober, Lester seemed like a normal person. But after a few drinks, his conversation would detour from work-talk to subjects more bizarre, like rescuing turtles from traffic fatalities. Sometimes Lester would share his philosophy.

There were two things he couldn't stand—men who smoked pipes and men who wore beards. He considered both of these practices pretentious. Men who did these things, Lester said, were "phony bastards," and "losers." Charlie had been wearing a beard for about a month.

As if reading Charlie's mind, Lester turned from the fish tank to look at his son-in-law. Either his expression indicated contempt, or he was about to throw up. Charlie couldn't tell which.

"Soon you'll be smoking a goddamn pipe," Lester said.

Linda glanced at Charlie with a look that said, "Don't answer, he's baiting you. He wants to pick a fight."

Charlie understood. He nodded, acknowledging Linda's unspoken message. He knew better than to provoke his father-in-law when he was drinking. Tonight, Lester seemed to be looking to battle, and Charlie decided that he wouldn't give Lester the satisfaction.

"Can I let the dog in?" Martha asked sheepishly.

"No," Lester snapped, turning his attention from

Charlie to Martha. "Keep the goddamn thing outside." He looked back at his fish tank. "I don't want your dog crapping on my rug."

Charlie felt like he was suffocating. The hairs from his mustache were blocking his nasal passages. Forcing a finger into each nostril, he pushed the hairs down so that he could open his airways. A few days ago he had been thinking about shaving so he could breathe better, but he felt that the mustache and beard made him look distinguished. *So what if I'm having trouble breathing?* He thought—*big deal.*

"You wanted the dog," Martha whined, addressing her husband. "You bought him."

"I bought him for you," replied Lester. "You said you were lonely."

Martha looked like she was about to cry. "I *was* lonely," she whimpered. "The same thing is happening all over again. Just when I get attached to a pet, you decide it has to go. I don't understand why you have to do this to me. Besides," she continued, "he has never crapped on the rug. He doesn't do that. He's a good boy." She hung her head, pouting like a child.

Lester lay on the floor and rolled onto his back. He closed his eyes, breathing so heavily that Charlie thought he had finally fallen asleep.

The narrator on television was talking about "a stockman's knife." He said it was a "collector piece with an abalone handle. It is one of the all-time most collected patterns." The announcer gave the item number, and Charlie wondered whether or not anyone ever bought these things. *This is probably a popular show with serial killers,* Charlie thought.

Martha got up from her seat and looked down at her husband. Then she walked to the kitchen, with Linda following behind.

Charlie looked at his father-in-law, who was now snoring loudly. *He looks like a blowfish.* Charlie thought. *With his skinny legs and arms sticking out and that enormous belly, he looks just like a blowfish all puffed up.* Charlie's thoughts were interrupted by the sound of Martha moving things around in the kitchen. He figured his mother-in-law was trying to decide whether or not to let her dog into the house.

"Do you think I can bring Brutus in now?" he heard Martha ask.

"Mother," Linda answered, "you don't really think he's gotten better, do you?"

Charlie understood the question was rhetorical. It referred to Lester's disappearance last night and tonight's drinking episode.

"I think he's improved," Martha whined. "He didn't mean to be late."

"He wasn't late, Mother. He wasn't there. He didn't show up. Remember?"

"He said he ran into an old friend," Martha said.

"Sure he did," replied Linda. "An army buddy, I suppose."

"He hasn't done anything like that in a long time. I think he's gotten better."

"Go ahead, let the dog in," Linda said. "He's asleep. He won't know if Brutus is inside the house or not."

A few moments later, the dog managed to free itself from its tether and bounded into the living room. Martha and Linda were in pursuit. It was a big dog, a Neapolitan Mastiff, who tended to drool excessively. He immediately ran up to Lester and began licking his face. Lester woke up suddenly and started to thrash around, swinging his arms and kicking out in all directions. When the dog backed off, Lester sat up. He appeared dazed and disoriented and began wiping his face with his hand.

"What the hell," he yelled. Then, seeing Martha, he turned on his wife. "Get that goddamn beast out of the house. He's slobbering all over me!"

As she and Linda began to chase Brutus around the room, Martha apologized. "I'm sorry, dear. I don't know how he got away. I was going to keep him in the kitchen, but somehow he got off his leash."

The dog jumped onto the couch and then off. He circled the room with the two women chasing behind.

Finally, Martha grabbed him and the animal pulled her half across the room. It was like trying to hold on to a locomotive. "I'll put him back in the kitchen, dear. Don't worry about him. You just rest now."

Lester didn't say anything. As soon as Brutus was out of the room, he lay back down on the floor. In a moment he was snoring again.

Marriage sucks, Charlie thought. *I ought to buy one of those god damn knives so I can cut my throat.* He was thinking this when Martha and Linda returned to the living room. Linda held a bowl of potato chips. They stepped over Lester, being careful not to disturb him. Whenever Lester was unconscious, the women always acted as if he wasn't present.

"Here, sweetie," Linda said, holding the bowl towards her husband. "Would you like some chips?"

Charlie's mother-in-law smiled at him. The sadness in her face was gone, and she almost looked happy. "How about a beer, Charlie? Would you like a tall boy? They're cold."

"Thank you," Charlie replied, reaching out to take the beer.

The man on the television was holding out a Samurai sword. "It's a genuine Katana," the man said.

Charlie wondered if that was the type of sword or the brand name and why a person would need a Samurai sword in today's world. He wondered how many ninja's were out in TV land ordering swords. He wasn't sure, and he really didn't care. It was getting late, and Charlie was sleepy. All he knew was that somewhere in Michigan a turtle was crossing the road. The animal needed assistance, and he probably wasn't going to get it—at least, not tonight.

Jim Pahz

EASTER SURPRISE*

Although there were beautiful churches and synagogues close to home, Daniel Fisher's family never attended any of them. Religion was an unopened door in the Fisher household, a room they never entered. Daniel's mom, Daphne had come from the south where she had been raised as a Baptist. Daniel's dad, Abe, was Jewish or was once Jewish a long time ago. But now neither parent was religious, although they considered themselves to be spiritual people. Being an interfaith couple they wanted to be enlightened and respectful of all faiths. To others who questioned their approach, Daniel's parents had an answer: "We believe in tolerance."

Daphne and Abe wanted their children to accept both Christianity and Judaism as moral foundations. When they met complaints from either side of the family, they calmly explained: "Our children are free to discover their own path to God, whatever that path may be."

Their children, however, were far too busy being children to discover any path. So, in the Fisher home the two religions merged haphazardly, forming a crazy quilt of ideas and practices. Hanukah, Christmas, Passover, and Easter, Santa Claus, the Easter Bunny, Jesus, and Moses were all part of the same colorful tapestry, with Tinker Bell and the Tooth Fairy thrown in for good measure. Judaism and Christianity were equally and superficially acknowledged.

This approach worked while the children were babies, but proved insufficient, as they grew older. The interfaith dilemma first became a problem when Daniel was ten years old. He and his younger brother Michael were enrolled in the Woodlawn Academy, a private elementary school for boys. Woodlawn was associated with the Episcopal Church. The boys wore a uniform that consisted of a white shirt and red tie, beneath a blue blazer. On the left pocket of the blazer, over the heart, was a white shield divided into quarters by a conspicuous red cross. In each quadrant of the shield were intriguing symbols. Daniel was in fifth grade and his brother Michael in the first.

Daniel had been working on an assignment for school. He was supposed to investigate birds and write a report on one he particularly liked. He researched his assignment by examining *National Geographic* magazine and several others, including *The Journal of the Audubon Society.* It was a difficult choice. He thought about the American eagle because it was the national bird. The robin was a contender because it heralded spring, and he recently found a dead robin in his driveway. Eventually he chose the quetzal bird because he thought it was the most beautiful bird in the world. This bird was special. When he first gazed upon a picture of the quetzal it seemed to call to him from the pages of the magazine. It was as if he recognized it, even though he had never seen a quetzal before. So, on a Wednesday afternoon a few days before Easter, Daniel was ready to present his report on the quetzal bird to the class. When his turn came he proudly stood in front of the class with his exhibits. He had drawn and colored an impressive quetzal bird on poster board alongside a crude map of Central America. The poster leaned on an easel beside him as he addressed the class. He held his written report in his hands. It was not necessary for him to read it because he had committed it to memory. He looked out at his classmates and took a deep breath, as his mother had advised during practice sessions at home. Then he began:

"The quetzal is one of the most beautiful birds in the world. It is the national bird of Guatemala. The original people of Guatemala were called the Maya. They thought a lot about the quetzal. It is a pretty bird with shining colors. His blue and green and red feathers have a sheen and glitter that make him very beautiful. The Mayan chiefs thought the quetzal bird was their spiritual protector. In Guatemala it is against the law to hunt the quetzal. The bird can't live in captivity. If you confine a beautiful quetzal bird to a birdcage, it will die. That is why this bird is a symbol of freedom. It must be free to live. The quetzal lives in the cloud forests of Central America in the countries of Guatemala and Costa Rica. What is the future of the quetzal bird? I don't know. Some scientists say it's in danger of becoming extinct. That means it may die. It's disappearing because man is cutting

down all the trees and destroying the natural habitat of the bird. I hope the quetzals don't all die, because they are beautiful birds."

Daniel was proud of his report and relieved when he finished the presentation without any mistakes. At its conclusion the teacher, Mrs. Odykirk, stood at her desk and said, "Thank you, Mr. Fisher. Does anyone have any questions for Mr. Fisher?"

Daniel liked Mrs. Odykirk, a short woman with a happy, round face. She always wore pink lipstick and lots of costume jewelry. As usual, her blonde hair was pulled neatly back from her face and twisted into a bun. Today she wore a collection of Bakelite bangles on her wrists that rivaled the quetzal in their color and brilliance. As she spoke to the class, gesturing with her hands, Daniel could imagine a quetzal flitting around the room. One hand waved at the back of the class, and Mrs. Odykirk called on Brian Miller.

"What color are the quetzal bird's eggs?" Brian asked.

Mrs. Odykirk turned to Daniel, her eyes wide with

curiosity. "An excellent question. Can you tell us anything about the quetzal's eggs, Mr. Fisher?"

"Yes," Daniel replied, thrilled to be able to provide the answer. "The quetzal lays two blue eggs."

"How lovely," Mrs. Odykirk said. "That reminds me of the Easter eggs some of you will be hunting on Sunday. Thank you, Mr. Fisher. You may sit down now." Daniel grabbed his quetzal poster and headed to his desk while Mrs. Odykirk began to tell the Easter story.

Mrs. Odykirk was a good storyteller. Although she was small, she was dynamic, with an expressive voice and face. Now that Daniel had finished his report, he could relax. He vaguely knew about Easter but had stopped believing in the Easter Bunny, so instead of listening to Mrs. Odykirk, he was reliving the success of his report and watching the quetzal bangles on her wrists swing back and forth as she flung her arms for emphasis.

"Of course," she said, her voice now lowered to gain her students' full attention, "not everyone believes in Easter." She paused to let this idea sink in. "Not everyone believes that our Lord and Savior arose from the dead. Some people don't believe in Jesus. Can you imagine? Does anyone know which people don't believe in Jesus or that he arose from the dead?"

Silence. No hands were raised.

"Well, I will tell you. Jewish people don't believe that Jesus was the Son of God. That's one group. Jewish people pray differently. They read and write backwards. They even speak in a different language when they pray in their church. Their language is called Hebrew." She smiled and looked around the room cheerfully.

"Actually, we have a Jewish boy in our classroom. Daniel Fisher is Jewish, I believe. Is that right, Mr. Fisher?"

The sound of his name broke Daniel's reverie, and he stiffened in his chair, suddenly aware that all eyes were on him—and not in appreciation for his quetzal report. He tried to think of the correct answer, but Mrs. Odykirk didn't wait for a response.

"Can you speak to us in Hebrew?" she asked. "Or maybe you can recite some of those funny-sounding chants?"

She smiled widely.

Daniel could feel himself blush and realized that he must be turning red. He wanted to jump up and dart from the room, but he felt like he had been nailed to the seat and wasn't sure what to do. Was he Jewish? He didn't know the answer. He knew that his father was Jewish, and his grandparents, Papa Dave and Nana Hannah, were Jewish. They were from Romania and spoke with an accent. Sometimes they spoke Yiddish, with musical words that Daniel liked; words like *chochkee, mishuggah*, and his favorite, *keezilmazallah*. These were "old country" words. Was Yiddish the same as Hebrew? He didn't know.

His mother's family was different. They were Baptist, which he knew meant that they were Christian and believed in Jesus. But what religion did this make him? He realized he had to say something. Everyone was now staring at him as they waited for his answer. He felt like a bird trapped in a cage. On the verge of desperation, he realized that, in addition to everything else that had gone wrong, he was beginning to sweat. Then in his head he heard his mother's voice stating the answer she always gave when relatives talked about religion, and he repeated her words: "We believe in tolerance."

That answer seemed to break the spell. His classmates then turned their scrutiny to Mrs. Odykirk, who had lost her smile. Daniel could breathe again, and the prickly sensation was going away, but he was still troubled. He didn't fully understand what had just happened, but he didn't like Mrs. Odykirk so much any more. She really wasn't a nice person although her quetzal bracelets were pretty. He was going to ask his parents about tolerance when he got home. He needed to know whether tolerance was Christian or Jewish.

Later that afternoon, he told his mother about his troubling day. He told her how good he had felt about the quetzal report, and then described, as best he could, the episode in which Mrs. Odykirk asked if he was Jewish. "She wanted me to chant, but I didn't know how," he said. "I was scared because I didn't know what to say, so I just told her that we believe in tolerance."

"What did Mrs. Odykirk say to that?" Daniel's mom

asked casually.

Daniel shrugged. "Nothing. She said we needed to get into our science groups because we didn't have much time to finish our projects." He paused, looking at her intently. "What is tolerance?"

"We'll talk about that when your father gets home." Daphne was putting milk and cookies on the table. "Can you get Michael?" Mom asked Daniel. "Go and find your brother." While Daniel was gone, Daphne tacked the quetzal poster on the wall in the breakfast nook, where it could be appreciated while they had their afternoon snack.

That evening, after Abe arrived home, Daniel's parents talked for a long time. Daniel was asked once again to explain what occurred at school. Daniel told them, adding his suspicions about Mrs. Odykirk. "I don't think she's a nice person," he said. "I think maybe she doesn't like me because I'm Jewish like you, Dad. Am I?" His parents smiled sympathetically, and his dad gave him a hug.

"Daniel, you're lucky because you can be whatever you want to be. You can be Jewish if you want, or you can be

Christian. Nobody, not even Mrs. Odykirk, can decide that for you."

"But I don't know what I want to be."

"That's okay. You can take all the time you want. Some people spend their whole lives trying to decide."

That wasn't what Daniel wanted to hear. He would have preferred a quick answer. Even having someone like Mrs. Odykirk telling him what to be seemed better than trying to decide for himself.

"Daniel," his dad continued. "Your mom and I think that maybe we can find a better school for you and Michael, one where people are more tolerant."

"What does that word mean?" Daniel asked.

"It means that the teachers will be nice. They will treat you better. Not like Mrs. Odykirk."

"And Daniel," Mom added quickly. "We think it's time we get a dog."

Daniel couldn't believe his ears. He had been asking for a dog for more than two years and was always told, "No, a dog is too much work."

"You're older now. If you'd be willing to help care for it, we think you and your brother Michael are ready."

"Wow! Thank you, Mom." *What a confusing day*, he thought. After all that had happened, he was getting a dog, and in a weird way he had Mrs. Odykirk to thank for it.

Mom and Dad kept their word. The following week, Daniel and Michael were enrolled in Public School 109. When Michael first heard the news, he was upset.

"I like Woodlawn," Michael said, "especially the uniforms. They don't have uniforms in the new school." Even so, Michael wanted the dog as much as Daniel. Changing schools was a small price to pay for a dog.

The puppy was waiting for them when they got up Easter morning.

"Did the Easter Bunny bring him?" Michael asked.

"Yes," his mother replied. "He brought it for you and your brother because you're such good boys."

AND THE WORLD GOES BOOM

His name was Saeed Meshkak, and he was from Iran, a country with a mysterious and romantic past. Think magic carpets. It was spring semester and Dr. Meshkak was on a Fulbright Faculty Exchange. He must have been surprised when he got off the plane in Lansing. He may have thought spring semester meant warm sunny weather, but Michigan in January is anything but spring-like. It is cold and there is usually a lot of snow.

I remember him as a small man who stood about 5 foot 4 inches tall. He was polite, but formal, and I was surprised when I received an invitation to his house warming. He had been here for only a few weeks, and his home, a three-bedroom ranch, was a rental. I, myself, was also new to the university, just starting my academic career.

It was exceptionally frigid on the day of the party, and there was about a foot of snow. The guests arrived within minutes of each other. They milled about in front of the stoop outside the front door. A woman, I assumed to be Mrs. Meshkak, stood on the stoop greeting the guests one at a time. She was a thin woman with long black hair and angular features. She stood at least two inches taller than her husband. The group of guests formed themselves into a line as they waited to gain entrance.

My wife Barbara and I were almost to the front of the line when a small boy four or five years old came outside. The child held a roller skate, not the kind you see today, but one of the old-fashioned metal kinds. He said something to the woman, who answered back in a language I assumed was Farsi. Apparently, whatever she said displeased the boy, and he hurled the roller skate at her, hitting her squarely in the chest and knocking her flat on her back into the snow. Then the child screamed something and ran into the house.

The woman appeared stunned as a couple of other guests and I helped her back on her feet. She didn't show signs of any physical damage, but she was out of breath and clearly embarrassed.

"I am sorry," she sputtered, brushing snow off

her sweater. "Please to forgive little boy, who is my son, Mohammed. Sometimes little boy get angry."

Upon entering the house I saw an open floor plan. The living room was large and in the corner was a fireplace in which a fire was burning. There were trays of hors d'oeuvres and beverages set out on a table for guests.

The people were milling around, making polite conversation. After about twenty minutes the child appeared again. This time he was holding a shopping bag, and he reached into the bag and withdrew a tiny plastic figurine. Then, looking around the room, he hurled the toy. It struck one of the guests. The child laughed and withdrew another from the bag. He threw it in a different direction. The person in its path saw it coming and leaned to the side. The projectile missed the guest and bounced off the wall.

By now, the visitors were all watching the child and the sound level of conversation in the room diminished. The boy continued to reach into his bag and get figures— cowboys, Indians, and plastic horses. He hurled them randomly at guests. Nobody demanded he stop. Not one person addressed either parent. I wanted to say something and thought (as I'm sure most people did) *"What the hell is wrong with your kid?"* But I didn't. Probably nobody spoke because criticizing someone for how they parent a child is a sensitive matter, even if you know the people well. In this case the professor and his family were guests of our university, our community, and our country. Furthermore, there was the whole cultural sensitivity thing and how we should all treat one another with respect and appreciate differences. A diversity appreciation dinner was scheduled on the university docket for later in the week. Maybe it was normal for kids in Iran to behave so badly. I didn't know and I doubted whether the other guests did. So, I assume, for these reasons, we all remained silent and allowed ourselves to be targets for little Mohammed Meshkak.

As he threw his plastic cowboys and Indians, many people swerved to the side or ducked to avoid being hit. This seemed to annoy little Mohammed who would frown every time he missed a target. Finally, when his bag was empty and there was nothing left to throw, the boy stood alone and downcast. People stopped paying attention to him and went back to making small talk with one another.

But the child wasn't finished. In a last effort to recapture everyone's attention the little boy ran to the fireplace and jumped into the fire, then, immediately leaped out. His pants were actually smoking. Once again, all eyes were focused on him, and the room was absolutely quiet, except for a few gasps and one or two softly spoken epithets. Suddenly, as if awakened from a dream, his mother sprang to life. She grabbed the child's arm and pulled him into the kitchen, all the while apologizing to her guests.

"Little boy set pants on fire. I don't know why little boy do this thing. Please to forgive."

I remember thinking, *now the child will get what he deserves*. I expected (I'm sure everyone did) the child would wail as his mother began to give him a well-deserved spanking. But nothing happened—absolute silence, what they call a pregnant pause. Then, after a few moments, the little boy wandered back into the living room followed by his mother. He was carrying a 2-liter bottle of Coca-Cola with a long straw extending from the bottle to the child's mouth. The bottle was almost as big as he was. He carried it by wrapping both arms around it and pressing it against his chest and belly. Mrs. Meshkak continued to apologize to the guests in broken English as she followed him back into the living room.

"Please to excuse little boy," she said. "Mohammed must to have three or four bottles of Coke each day or he is not being happy child. If boy gets upset he grinds teeth. Doctor says not good thing to do. Healthy mouth is same as healthy child. Not need to be Coke, you understand, Pepsi or Dr. Pepper okay. Even the Mountain Dew our Mohammed is liking. What should I do? He must to have these beverages to be happy boy."

I'm sure everyone understood, though I doubt if many sympathized. I began to calculate. *The child weighs approximately 40 pounds. He drinks 3 or 4 giant bottles of cola. Each cola contains approximately 25 milligrams of caffeine and maybe 30 grams of sugar.* Assuming he drinks 3 bottles, that totals a lot of caffeine and even more sugar. I had to smile. I had solved the mystery of the fire hopper. Like Sherlock Holmes, I deduced the reason the boy acted like a psychotic squirrel crossing the highway. He was drugged! Of course it only made things worse that his parents appeared to be completely lacking the most rudimentary parenting skills and their child was a brat. That was obvious. Professor Meshkak may have been brilliant in the classroom, but he didn't know much about disciplining a child.

In retrospect, the fire leaping episode was the high point of the party. Things went down hill after that. As they say, it was a hard act to follow. Soon people began to express their appreciation to the hosts, thanking them for their invitation and making their escape.

*   *   *

I didn't see Dr. Meshkak again for several weeks. I worked in a different academic department. One day, towards the end of the semester, I passed him in the hall and stopped to speak with him.

"Dr. Meshkak," I said. "How are you?"

"Not so well," he replied.

"I'm sorry. What's wrong?"

"My son was expelled from kindergarten."

"What?" I was thinking: *How does a child get expelled from kindergarten? All they do there is play.*

"Yes," Meshkak said. "They told his mother not to bring him back to the school. Mrs. Kelly, the principal, say Mohammed's behavior disruptive to learning environment."

"I see. What will you do?"

"We return home soon to Iran. In two months. Mohammed is good boy… intelligent child. Maybe little boy drink too much beverage."

"Oh, you think so?"

"Yes, boy's mother says he can be difficult child so she give him pop cola. I am thinking to keep him home with mother until we return to Iran. Boy can begin school again in Iran."

I thought for a moment of telling him my conclusions about his son's caffeine and sugar consumption. And I wanted to compliment his wife on her insightfulness. But then I thought, *what's the point? He's leaving in a month.*

Why make him feel worse than he already does? So I didn't say anything, except to wish him a good day. Then I went on my way.

I never saw Dr. Meshkak or his family again. Apparently they returned to Iran when the semester ended. I forgot about them for a long time.

* * * *

One night, many years later, I was watching the news on television with Barbara. An aid worker with a non-governmental agency had been kidnapped in Iran. The network was making a big deal about it. The camera panned in on the crowds in the street. People were screaming all kinds of things. Some were self-flagellating with chains. One scruffy-looking young man being interviewed spoke in broken English about Jihad, Palestinians, and Zionist aggression. He was saying how the aid worker was captive as punishment for world injustice, which he blamed on Israel and the great Satan (guess who?). Behind him an effigy of Uncle Sam was hanging over a fire. His pants were smoking.

"Fruitcakes-R-Us," I mumbled to Barbara.

She was staring intently at the television set. "Do you know who that man reminds me of, the one giving the interview?"

"Who?"

"That little kid who was so badly behaved—the one who jumped into the fire."

"You mean Mohammed Meshkak, the Coke sucker?"

"Yeah, that one."

"Impossible. It was too long ago."

"It is possible. He's grown up. It would make him about 20-25 years old. You've got to admit the guy looks like him."

"Perhaps. He is short enough, but he could be anybody, even one of the seven dwarfs."

"I don't think the child ever cut down on his intake of caffeine. He's an angry- looking dude."

I looked closer and tried to focus my eyes. I couldn't tell. "You don't suppose it could really be that little fire hopper?"

"Anything is possible," Barbara said. "After all, people win the lottery every week, and what are the odds of that happening? Look, I believe the guy is grinding his teeth."

"Well, that settles it. It probably is little Mohammed. I remember his mother said he did grind those choppers. Too bad the guy doesn't have a bag of toys to throw at people. It might help him to make his point, whatever that is."

Suddenly there was an explosion. Boom. The camera went haywire with images appearing sideways and out of focus. Then the picture was gone and the television went blank.

My wife and I sat stunned, staring at the empty screen in disbelief, waiting to see what would happen next. Then, after two or three minutes, the picture returned and a new announcer appeared. The video showed carnage left from the explosion with smoke and fire. The announcer said:

"A terrible tragedy… an incendiary device of some kind. A great deal of damage."

"Holy cow!" Barbara said. "Did you see that?

*   *   *

For the rest of the evening there was talk of nothing else on the television except the incident in Iran. Several people had been killed including the hostage, an American journalist, and several Iranian students. No group came forward to claim responsibility. Nothing was said of the identity of the student being interviewed before the explosion or whether or not he was the bomber. On the streets of Tehran, people who were interviewed expressed their idea that the only one to blame for the incident was the United States—the great Satan.

*   *   *

During dinner I turned to Barbara and said, "That boy became infected."

"Infected?"

"Yes, like with a virus, Somehow this person's personal discontent merged with politics. In his delusional state he believed he could be an instrument to make the world a better place and he would gain instant access to paradise at the same time.

Young male Muslims,

dying to die.

Choosing martyrdom

For pie in the sky."

"How do you make the world better by killing people? Especially innocent people like women and children."

"You don't. Unless your mind is infected and then you think you will. And our little friend, or somebody else's little friend, was terminally infected."

"And so the world goes boom," Barbara said,

"Yes, and the TV ratings go up, and pundits talk and say obvious things like: 'Couldn't anyone see this coming? Weren't there any red flags? He left his internet postings for the world to see.'"

"And you think little Mohammed was one of those people?"

"Who knows? Probably not, but stranger things have happened."

"And so, the world goes boom."

Jim Pahz

COTTON BALLS

When I arrived at Earl's mobile home I found him sitting at a table. He was a tall, good looking fellow with chiseled features. As usual he was wearing a western outfit—jeans, boots, and a black cowboy hat. This time, however, he also wore latex gloves. He was spooning white powder into envelopes.

"What are you doing?"

"Anthrax."

"What?" I asked.

"The bank. I'm going to kill it."

"What bank?"

"Third Fifth Bank, the one on the south end of town."

"You can't be serious."

"You see the powder, don't you?"

I looked more closely around the room, trying to grasp what was going on. It was like my brain was out of focus. I shook my head to clear the confusion.

"Wait a minute," I said. "That's Johnson's Baby Powder."

"So?"

"So, it's not anthrax."

"No," Earl said. "It's a practice session, a dress rehearsal."

"You're going to send anthrax to the bank, like the person on the news a few years ago?"

"That's right."

"But why?"

"Because I hate that bank and all the thieves who work there."

"You hate them enough to kill them?"

"That's right. They robbed me. It was a legal robbery, but they robbed me nevertheless. I intend to take my revenge."

"Earl," I said. "You're talking like a crazy person. What could these people have done to make you want to kill them?"

Earl looked up and turned his chair to face me. Then he removed his hat and began his story.

"Last month I went to Philadelphia," he said, "to see my sister, Susan. She's pretty comfortable, financially I mean. She and her husband have this big house in Blue Bell, this really affluent suburb outside of Philadelphia. Her kids are grown and out of the nest, and there's plenty of room. Her husband works hard and is frequently away. So my sister says to me, 'Earl, stay as long as you want. I enjoy your company. Stay awhile.' So I did. I stayed a couple of weeks, and I had a really good time. My sister's a great woman.

"But, I guess, before I left home, I miscalculated the balance in my checking account. According to my records I had some money in the account. But the bank said otherwise. They said I was overdrawn by fifty cents. I didn't know this until I returned from Philadelphia and picked up my mail from the post office. There were two letters from the bank. The first informed me they were charging me thirty dollars for my fifty-cent overdraft. The second said I was being fined six dollars each day for having a negative balance in my account.

"I went to the bank the next day and explained I had been out of town and my mail had been held at the post office. So, I really hadn't been notified. I also told them I checked my telephone messages each day to see if there was anything important I needed to be concerned with. There were no messages from the bank. I think that is important.

"The woman I spoke with, Carolyn something, said, 'Oh that's unfortunate, because the calls from the bank are automated. If our machine reaches a voice mail it cuts off. It only leaves a message if someone actually answers the phone.' The woman smiled at me and said how sorry she was. Then she said it would take $150 to close the account and if I paid it then I could save the six-dollar fine that would be charged for today. I could tell she was enjoying herself.

"I closed the account. What choice did I have? I told her she and her colleagues should be ashamed. You are the bad guys, I said. You're worse than the people that rob banks. You're like the sheriff of Nottingham, stealing from your own people. As I stormed out of the bank, I told them

I hoped they got what they deserved, and it sure wasn't a financial bailout from the government. What really bothers me is all that bailout money, that seven or so billion dollars they want. It's our tax money. Some of it is my tax money, and I sure don't want it to go to no bank. Especially banks that treat customers like Third Fifth does. Anyway, by the time I reached my car I had decided I would see that the bastards got what was coming to them."

Earl paused, looking at me intently as he removed the gloves and put his hat back on. Then he asked, "What exactly is Anthrax, anyway?"

*   *   *

My friend Earl wasn't a crazy person, even though sometime he acted like it. At least I didn't think he was. Usually he was the nicest, most soft-spoken, and likable individual one could imagine. But it hadn't been a good year for him. I knew that, and as I looked around the rusty old mobile home that he was now renting, I sympathized.

When I first met Earl, he seemed to have everything: a decent job, married, and loving family. But shortly afterward, his wife got sick. She developed kidney failure and later was diagnosed with Lupus. As far as Earl went, you never saw a more attentive husband. He would carry Phyllis when she needed to be moved from one place to the next. He doted on her and even learned how to cook. Anything he could do to make life better for Phyllis he would do. There were a few months when Phyllis was in crisis and the family believed they were going to lose her, and during that time it was Earl who was the rock that everybody leaned on. And then Phyllis began to recover, physically at least. But as she recovered she became cantankerous. She was hard to get along with.

That's when Earl got involved with horses. Maybe the animals were a distraction, a way to avoid his wife's bad disposition. Or maybe they were a way to live out a long-standing fantasy. But Earl started to buy more and more horses and spend more time in the barn with them.

The Hoffmeyers lived in the country. Earl had previously worked for the auto industry during the evenings. In addition to building cars, he built most of his home himself during his off hours. But that was before Phyllis got sick and the horses came. Earl never met a horse he didn't like. For the most part his horses were quarter horses—the horse that built America. The first ones Earl purchased were pleasure horses for riding. Later he began to expand his operation by buying racing stock. Earl never actually raced a horse, but he had plans.

The idea of a horse completed Earl unlike any other man I have ever known. It gave him his identity, a modern version of the cowboy. He began to dress in western wear, always wearing a cowboy hat and boots. He started hanging out at the Saint Johns Horse Auction, and every other Saturday morning you could find him at the sale, where he became a permanent fixture. He stood inside the sales ring like a professional horse trader. He never sat in the bleachers where the customers sat. Usually, he leaned against a rail with a piece of straw sticking out of his mouth. He could have been the Marlboro Man. He not only looked the part, he lived it. I think Earl believed he was a cowboy.

Even Earl's home took on a western flavor: lamps, wall hangings, pictures, everything had the western motif.

He kept acquiring more and more horses, and by the time I got to know him, Earl had about twenty. He named his home place The Little Ponderosa and installed an entrance made from logs where his driveway began. It was done on a grand scale, even though his house, barn, and everything else sat on a mere seven acres.

Unfortunately, it wasn't long before the appearance of his homestead changed from looking like a postcard to that of a scene from the Michigan Livestock Exchange. Earl was weak on chores that would keep the place tidy. Manure piled up in the barn and paddocks. Earl didn't seem to care that after a rainy day a person (or a horse) walking in a corral would sink up to their knees in the muck. The smell of horse manure was pervasive.

But if Earl didn't care, Phyllis did. She began to complain about the horses and grew to hate them. Once when I was visiting, Phyllis got angry and started to tongue lash her husband.

"The stink and the cost. That's what I object to." She complained, "Not to mention the work. Why," she asked, "does anyone need twenty horses? We don't live in Montana, and you aren't going on a cattle drive. All our discretionary income is going into the care and feeding of these animals. I don't know if you realize it or not, but it's expensive to keep horses. There is food and hay to buy, veterinary expenses, blacksmith fees, and stakes payments for the horses you have never raced. I don't want to disillusion you, Earl, but you are not a cowboy and this isn't Lonesome Dove, and we're broke. Even with your clothing and hats, you are just an unemployed automotive worker who can't or won't live on a budget. Who knows if you will ever get employment again, and how are we going to pay off these credit card debts?"

"You're right. I'm not a cowboy." He paused for a few moments while reflecting, then said, "I'm a horseman." His wife looked at him as if he was insane. She shook her head and threw up her hands. "Whatever," she replied and stormed out of the room.

It was sometime shortly after that incident that Phyllis hired a man who lived down the street to come and do chores, which meant he was mostly mucking stalls.

The man's name was Randy and he lived at his home with his parents. Randy was also unemployed and said he liked to do farm work, and he worked cheap. Earl didn't mind, at least not at first. Randy was about eleven years younger than Phyllis. Earl found his wife's complaints tedious. He resented her nagging. But he also realized he had better do something to add to the family income.

These events happened in Michigan from about 2005 until the time Chrysler filed for bankruptcy protection. It was an era when the automotive industry was really starting to implode. The economy was in recession, and plants were closing everywhere. Not just the ones that built cars, but all ancillary services as well. Anything connected with the car industry was in trouble. Earl lost his job and after Phyllis became ill with Lupus she was forced to give up her position at Walmart and go on disability.

So to raise extra money Earl began to rent out stalls in his barn. He actually got a few boarders. Since Randy had begun working, the barn was clean and didn't look bad at all.

One of his customers was an attractive woman named Bunny. She would come over every other day to see about her horse and to exercise him. She and Earl became good friends and they began riding horses together. Bunny was in her thirties, had red hair and freckles and a nice figure. But more importantly, she had a pleasant disposition and was not like Earl's wife, Phyllis, who he described as "a rank mare." Bunny began coming to see about her horse first thing in the mornings after her husband left for work. She and Earl spent a lot of time riding together.

One morning I was visiting Earl. He had called me saying he had a new horse he wanted to show me. After spending time visiting in the barn with Earl we walked back to his house. When we entered we found Randy sitting on a chair alongside of Phyllis and applying bright red nail polish to her toenails. I remember that each toe had a cotton ball between it and the next toe. I have never been able to get that image out of my mind.

Earl looked stunned. He didn't seem to know what to say, so he didn't say anything. He just stood there watching as if trying to decide if the color of the polish was the best color for these toes. I was embarrassed for him so I tried to make small talk. For a moment I though Earl might have a showdown. I tried to imagine what legendary cowboys like Tom Mix, Gene Autry, or John Wayne would do in a similar situation. But I don't think they would have acted like my friend, Earl. I took a hard look and realized that if Earl was going to do anything he might start to cry. I didn't want to see that so I suggested we take another look at that horse again.

"You think I'm a pussy, don't you?" Earl said, once we were outside the house.

"No… not exactly," I confessed. "A pussy might have been a little more forceful."

I later learned, after I returned home that Earl had gone to Bunny for advice. He wanted to know if she thought it was appropriate behavior for a hired hand to be painting his wife's toenails."

Bunny didn't think so. "A hired hand needs to be in the barn cleaning," she said.

Then she suggested they go riding to take his mind off his worries.

The weeks passed and apparently Randy's behavior became become more and more outrageous with respect to Phyllis. He now rubbed her back, dried her hair after she washed it, and who knows what else and all the time Earl acted like nothing was out of order. He became sullen and withdrawn. Whenever he was concerned he turned to Bunny for support and understanding.

"You know Earl," Bunny said one day. "I think Randy is too handy. You need to throw him out. You're the king of your castle. You need to protect what is yours. I think Randy and your wife are getting too close to one another."

"I know." Earl replied, "But I'm not sure how to handle it." So he continued to do nothing. He might have wanted to take bold, decisive action, but Earl was not only a cowboy, he was a procrastinator.

Finally when Earl worked up the courage to face his wife it was too late. Phyllis had decided what was to be done. "I want a divorce," she said. "Randy and I are in love."

"But he's the handy man, the hired help. He shovels shit, for heaven's sake. And he's too young for you. He's little more than a boy for heavens sake."

"Randy may be a handy man, but he is a man who knows how to treat a lady," Phyllis replied. "Besides, you have your horses and your little Bunny friend to play with. You know, your exercise buddy." She had a lot of sarcasm in her tone.

The divorce was granted on grounds of irreconcilable differences. Earl got plucked like a ranch chicken for the stew pot. Phyllis got the house, what little money there was, and almost everything else, except the horses. Earl got them. A short time after the divorce Phyllis and Randy were married.

Earl morphed into a different Marlboro man, the one who just learned he had lung cancer from all those cigarettes he had smoked through the years. He lost enthusiasm for everything. He rented a run-down mobile home on another person's property. The home was rusty and the roof leaked. One by one he sold off the horses and used the money for living expenses. Earl really loved those horses, so each time he sold one it was like suffering another body blow. He was simply beaten down and there was no joy left in his life whatsoever.

Bunny moved her horse to greener pastures. If it wasn't for the fact that the people who owned the property where Earl lived had a teenage daughter who loved horses, Earl never would have been able to go to Philadelphia and visit his sister. But Earl needed to go. The teenager agreed to feed the few animals Earl had left while Earl was away.

*　*　*

It might have been the greatest shock of my life, but at first I didn't see it. I had been sitting at my kitchen table eating a tuna fish sandwich and not paying any particular attention to the news playing in the background. When I turned the set on the commentator was saying, "He was a monster who wanted to set things straight in his own mind."

That was all I heard. Then the announcer went to another story. When I finished the sandwich, I got up and turned the set off. Same old stuff, just another day of gloom and misery. Later that night I turned the set on again and heard the announcer talking about the incident from the afternoon's news. But this time there was a picture of the monster—it was Earl, my friend. He wasn't wearing his cowboy hat.

The announcer said that Earl had entered the Third Fifth Bank carrying a shopping bag. He walked to the counter and waited in line for a teller. He stood quietly until it was his turn. Then he reached into the bag and pulled out a shotgun—a double barrel shotgun with the barrel shortened. He got off the first round knocking two tellers to the floor— the one in front of him, nearly cut in half, and the one behind her, who was working the drive-through window. Both were killed. His second blast downed a third teller. Then he reached into his belt and pulled out a pistol and ran into one of the offices and shot another employee, an assistant manager named Carolyn. By the time Earl was finished, he had killed six people. By then the SWAT team arrived and he was gunned down.

At the conclusion of the newscast the announcer offered his commentary.

"No demands for money were made by the killer. It's unclear what his motivation could have been." The announcer speculated. "The perpetrator must have been completely deranged. All we know for sure is a man named Earl Hoffmeyer behaved like a monster—thoughtless, and savage—a beast who went postal."

I sat there stunned. For a while I couldn't move. Then, when the thaw set in, I went to the bookcase and took out a dictionary. I looked up the word monster. It said, a person or animal that deviated from normal, acceptable ways of behaving. Well, I thought, that's Earl.

I wondered about my assessment of Earl. Could I have been so wrong about him? I would never have suspected he was capable of violence. Then I remembered the last time I saw him, sitting at his table with his hands covered in baby powder. He had hit bottom and he probably didn't care if he lived or died. He had lost Phyllis, his family, home, and job. He was living in a rusted old tin can with a leaky roof.

Yet, I didn't see it coming. All I saw was a man acting silly, playing with baby powder. That should have been a red flag, but I missed it completely.

So, Earl acted out another one of his fantasies. He exacted his revenge, on Carolyn and all the other bank employees. He went out with guns blazing. Of course, he hadn't made any demands for money. He wasn't looking for money. He was there to get even because he believed the bank had robbed him. Earl wanted revenge. That was the code of the cowboy. Don't let the bad guys get away with something untoward. Don't let them win. Unfortunately, by enacting his own justice, Earl had, himself, become the bad guy. I wondered if he realized that.

I thought I should call the media and explain what I knew about Earl. I would say he wasn't a bad man, despite what he did. And he wasn't a monster. He was usually a kind and likable fellow with a good sense of humor. He took great care of his wife when she was ill, and what did he get for his efforts? Earl was a fellow who felt like he had lost everything there was in life to live for. And on top of everything he was outraged over a third rate bank and their mean-spirited accounting practices. It was the proverbial final straw.

In addition to calling the media, I thought I would call Earl's sister, Susan. I would tell her how sorry I was for her loss and how Earl had told me he had a really good time when he visited her in Philadelphia and that he thought she was a terrific person. It might make her feel better.

These days, whenever I remember Earl I don't think of him as a crazy person or a bank robber—certainly not as a monster. I see him as a cowboy and a victim of circumstance. But still, I can't get that image of Phyllis' toes out of my mind—those toes with the bright red paint and those cotton balls holding them apart. And I will never forget the look on Earl's face. Then I remember the incident with the baby powder. And then I make my resolve. I say to myself that under no circumstance will I ever go anywhere near, or consider opening a bank account, at Third Fifth Bank.

Jim Pahz

PARADISE*

Grace loved Guatemala, and in particular Canoguitas, the little town where the mission was located. It was a magical place of undistilled beauty with intense colors that vibrated like a Van Gogh painting. There were the reds, oranges, purples and greens—especially the greens. The greens, silent and knowing, formed a dense backdrop for the hibiscus, gardenias and poinsettia that blazed brightly in the garden. Other flowers, exotic and unnamed, sprang from window boxes, along fences, and over walls throughout the town. Each morning as Grace walked outside, her senses were bombarded: the sky was a dense blue ocean atop dark green mountains; the sun felt like a warm hand on her back, and the wind was a tender kiss that carried the smell of wonderful fruit like cushiness, caspiroles, and mangos mingled with the hint of tortillas and spices.

Pigs and dogs wandered the dirt streets, and in the mission compound guineas, chickens and peacocks roamed freely. There were avocados, bananas, and coconuts in abundance, just waiting to be picked. She loved this village whose name translated as "little canoes." She had lived in Canoguitas for almost a decade, and though not born here, Grace knew this was where she belonged.

The road with no name that led to the mission was lined with small houses and little shacks with dirt floors and open doors. Inside, people slept in hammocks. Household sounds spilled into the streets: the familiar cry of a baby, a dog barking, the clatter of pans and pots during kitchen chores. Then it was quiet when the villagers left for work in the fields. No one locked their doors; they knew when they returned their house and belongings would be just as they had left them. Sometimes Grace thought she had come to the Garden of Eden. She lived in paradise.

But Guatemala was also a place of squalor. The poverty was the same today as Elmer, her father-in-law, said it had been forty years ago when he began the mission. Elmer had come to save souls. Grace came after she married Tommy, Elmer's son whom she had met while attending college.

For as long as Grace could remember, she had wanted to be a missionary. Now she was living her dream. But it was not always a good dream. Her husband had more than his share of weaknesses, and the missionary life wasn't all that easy. Even in paradise, things weren't perfect.

This day had been a day like any other. Grace was trimming the blue hydrangea bushes in front of her house when she noticed a young woman walking toward her down the road with no name. The woman was small in stature with fine features, and she waddled like a duck as she approached. She supported her large belly with her arms as she walked, as if carrying a basket of laundry. *She must be due any day*, Grace thought, setting the pruning shears on the ground. Grace swiped a stray strand of hair from her face and watched the woman approach. The woman, Grace realized, was actually quite young—a girl perhaps in her late teens. The stranger was pretty, but looked weary and unkempt. Her clothes were stained and tattered. The left shoe was falling apart, and her foot looked like a tongue peeking through brown leather lips. Grace sensed a weariness from within the girl, not from the exertion of walking but from the toll of living—as if the young woman had seen or done too much and now she needed to be unburdened. Grace thought, *whoever this is, I feel her weariness. This is what disappointment does, it grinds you down.*

The girl stopped a few yards from Grace. "May I greet from you my salutation," she said. "I search for man in charge of mission. I believe the name is Reverend Tuttle." The woman looked sadly at Grace as she struggled with her broken English. Something black streaked her dust-covered cheeks, but Grace couldn't tell if it was from sweat or tears.

"Reverend Tuttle is probably in the administration building," Grace replied and pointed across the compound to a building behind the woman in the direction she had come from. "That is the main office of the mission."

"No. I come from there. Not that old man. It is young old man."

Grace was puzzled. There was only one minister in the compound, but there were two men named Tuttle.

"The name I believe is Thomas," the woman continued, "like in Bible; one who doubts our Lord."

"Oh, you must mean Tommy, my husband." Grace could see the girl was struggling with English, so she spoke Spanish. "My husband is not here now. Is there something I can do for you?"

The girl paused for a moment as if considering her options, and then continued, "Well, I am hungry. I haven't eaten for a long time."

She seemed relieved to speak in Spanish, though Grace suspected her native tongue was Quiché or one of the other languages of the indigenous Mayan people.

"I am worried about the baby," she said. "If the mother does not eat properly, will that not hurt the baby?"

"Yes, I believe it could," Grace answered. "When are you due?"

"Soon. I do not know exactly, but my baby will come soon."

"What is your name?" Grace asked.

"Felicita Sian."

"Why are you here, Felicita? What brings you to this place?"

"To see the Reverend Thomas. I was told to come here, because the Reverend Thomas could help me." She turned her gaze downward toward the ground. "My father made me leave. He cannot support another mouth to feed. He said my pregnancy is shameful. I have nowhere to go. People told me about the Friendship Mission. I was told Reverend Thomas could help me."

"Who told you?"

"People. I do not remember who."

"And the baby's father? Where is he?"

"Gone. I don't know where. I do not even know who he is. I met him once; only one time, at a fiesta. The father is unknown."

Unknown? Grace thought, *What an odd thing to say. How can you not know who your baby's father is? Did someone, maybe a lawyer, tell her to use that word... unknown?* "Where are you from, Felicita? Where is your home?"

"Mazatenango."

Mazatenango was about four hours by car from the mission. For whatever reason, the girl had travelled far and must be exhausted. Grace rose to her feet and removed her gardening gloves. Then she smiled at Felicita and extended her hand. "Please, come into my house. I will have Marta prepare something to eat. We can wait together. My husband will be home later. But I think you should know he's not a minister; he's a program administrator. You shouldn't call him 'Reverend.' Most people just call him 'Tommy'."

*   *   *

When Tommy arrived later that evening, Grace and Felicita were resting in the courtyard. Felicita relaxed in a lounge chair and the two sipped lemonade. As soon as Tommy waked through the entrance, Felicita stood. She hung her head to avoid looking at him while Grace introduced the young woman.

"This is Felicita. She has been waiting for you," Grace explained.

"I was told that you could help me," Felicita said,

looking at her feet. "I am going to have a baby."

Tommy bent sideways to look at Felicita's face. "Our ministry can find a family for your child," Tommy said. "If that's what you want."

"Yes, Reverend, because I cannot keep this baby."

Grace sat passively observing. She had a nagging feeling that something unspoken was going on beneath the surface. *Has Tommy seen this woman before? Could he have coached her?* This was the third baby in six months to find its way to the mission. Grace had learned of the other two children through one of her maids. *What happened to those babies? Were there others?* Despite her questions, she said nothing.

Tommy motioned for Felicita to sit, and he took a seat across from her. The young girl sat rigidly as Tommy promised to provide for her upkeep and to take care of the baby after the birth. Felicita listened and nodded as Tommy talked.

"This is a very important decision, Felicita," Tommy said. "It must not be made lightly. Why don't you rest now?

You can sleep in a guesthouse and we will talk more about it tomorrow."

As Felicita nodded, Grace watched a small tear slide down the side of her face. In the candlelight it left a glistening scar. Slowly, Felicita rose from her seat. She smiled shyly as she said goodnight to Grace, and then turned to follow Marta and Tommy to one of the guest cottages. Grace remained behind, wondering about Felicita and what had just happened.

*   *   *

For the next few weeks Grace observed Felicita as the girl waddled through the compound, and the two of them frequently shared lemonade in the afternoon. Felicita spoke of her unborn baby with affection, and Grace wondered if she would really release the child for adoption after it was born.

"I know it will be a girl," Felicita said. "We have many girls in my family." Her smile was broader now and her skin glowed. Rested and cleaned, she hardly looked like the same girl who had earlier wandered into the compound.

Grace was struck by Felicita's natural beauty and gentle nature. Felicita reminded her of a wildflower.

"With you as her mother she will be a beautiful child," Grace said. "I'm sure of that."

Felicita smiled, but Grace sensed a sadness within the girl. She didn't push, but each day as she worked in her garden Grace prayed for Felicita. The baby was born at 2:00 in the morning. It was a girl, just as Felicita had predicted. When the doctor arrived he pronounced both healthy. The baby was kept in a separate room from Felicita, because she wasn't sure about seeing the baby. But Grace checked on the infant, and held her in her arms. Her heart opened to the child. "You are beautiful and petite, just like your mother," Grace whispered. "I think I like you very much."

Then Grace went to Felicita and sat by her side as she slept. When she awoke, the first thing Felicita asked was: "Did you see her?"

"Of course, she is so beautiful, just like you. She is as close to a perfect baby as any I have ever seen."

Felicita sighed, pleased.

"Do you want to see or hold her?" Grace asked.

Felicita shook her head. "No. It is best I do not. Mr. Tommy said it was a bad idea. I just want her to have a good family, a better life. I want good parents for her. Someone like you."

Grace smiled and embraced Felicita. The two women cried.

The next afternoon when Grace arrived for a visit, both Felicita and the baby were gone. Grace felt a profound emptiness and loss, as if suddenly all color had been drained from the world. No one had any answers for her, and she was on the verge of panic when she confronted her husband.

"What happened?" she asked. "Where are Felicita and the baby?"

Tommy seemed unconcerned. "I don't know," he shrugged. "Felicita left."

"What do you mean, she left?"

"She left. Gone. What's not to understand?"

"Did she walk? Did you drive her? Did she take a bus?"

"I don't know. I didn't drive her. I guess she took a bus."

"And the baby?"

"The baby's fine," Tommy said. "Don't worry."

"But where is she?"

"In foster care."

"What foster care? Since when does the mission have foster care?"

Tommy gave her a harsh look—the one he used with Guatemalan employees who overstepped their boundaries or with children who have misbehaved. "Stop questioning me, woman," he said, sternly. "I'm doing my job." Then he walked away.

* * *

Grace was beside herself. She needed to see what had become of Felicita's baby, but to do so she had to find the so-called foster care. Early the next morning she went to see her father-in-law, Elmer, the man who had started the mission forty years ago. Under his guidance the program had prospered. Although Tommy was officially in charge now,

Elmer remained involved with everything that went on. The mission was Elmer's lifeblood and he would never let go of it completely.

Elmer's appearance startled Grace, and she tried to recall his exact age. She realized, guiltily, that it had been several weeks since she had spoken with him. Today, he looked old—older than usual—and he seemed a little confused. She noted his frail, vulnerable appearance and thought: *I must mention to Tommy how poorly he looks.* Elmer was evasive with Grace, and reluctant to reveal any information. Still, she pressed him. Eventually she learned the mission had rented a house for foster care in the Rapado, a small cluster of buildings about eight miles away.

Elmer's directions were sketchy, but with enough solid detail that Grace was confident she could find the house. Elmer said the house was painted green and located behind a *milpah,* a patch of corn. The house was surrounded by a circle of rocks. The rocks were painted white and Elmer said there was a red and yellow hammock on the porch.

It took Grace almost two hours to locate the property.

Elmer forgot to mention that behind the cornfield was a grove of trees, and the house was nestled deeply within the grove. She had almost given up the search, assuming that Elmer was as confused as he appeared, when she decided to follow the two-track road which ran along the north side of an overgrown patch of what looked like an abandoned plot of corn. As she came to the end of the corn she caught a glimpse of the white stones and the house hidden within the trees. There was a red and yellow hammock on the porch, just like Elmer described. She stopped the car at the edge of the trees, and cautiously walked up the path. But as she approached she heard a baby whimpering, and she quickened her pace. Without stopping to knock, she pulled open the door and entered, following the sounds she assumed were from Felicita's baby.

Inside the house, she was overwhelmed at first by the heat and the stench of urine. She was vaguely aware of the sound of flies buzzing from somewhere, and she had to remind herself to breathe. Once her eyes adjusted to the dark, she put her hand over her nose and mouth and she continued into a room where she found three toddlers sharing a crib. One was the source of the whimpering she had heard, and the other two immediately began to howl when they saw her. Grace's eyes moved to a second crib where she saw two infants. One looked to be a few months old and the other was a newborn. Grace felt her heart jump—*Felicita's baby!* Without thinking, she charged toward the crib and scooped the baby into her arms. *Who could leave a baby in place like this?* "My goodness gracious," Grace murmured as tears welled in her eyes. She clutched the infant, and then stood stunned, gazing at the other children. "What's to be done? I can't hold you all." In an instant her sadness gave away to anger. "Hello!" she shouted, turning around. "Is anybody here?"

She heard a creak in the floorboards in an adjacent room and a young woman appeared in the doorway. She wore a stained, once-white cotton dress and a pair of blue flip-flops. The woman looked as if she had just been awakened. Her hair was uncombed and she had a wild appearance about her. She leaned against the doorway and looked annoyed as she beheld Grace holding the baby.

"Who are you?" Grace demanded.

The woman shrugged, "I was resting. The heat is terrible." Quick as a lizard she grabbed a fly from the air and crushed it in her fist. Then she slowly opened her hand to confirm her victory. She smiled and flicked the insect to the floor. "What do you mean, who am I? Who are you? Are you the mother?" She looked at Grace with tired, indifferent eyes.

"Of course not," Grace snapped. Several flies were circling her head, and Grace waved her hand over the baby's face to shoo them away. "Who do these children belong to?" Grace demanded.

"You don't know?" The woman replied, sullenly.

Grace was livid. She completely forgot about her Christian demeanor and snapped. "Who's in charge here?" She was in no mood for the woman's insolence.

"Señor Tommy pays me my money. He is the boss."

Grace noted the confident smirk on the woman's face. "This child is ill," she said, moving with the baby toward the door. "I am taking her home with me."

"Oh, no. You cannot do that." The woman was suddenly alert and wide-eyed. "Señor Tommy says nobody is supposed to come here. Nobody has anything to do with the children. It is a private matter. That is what he said."

"Well, I don't care what Señor Tommy said. I am Señora Tommy. Do you understand? I am his wife and I am taking this baby home with me right now. She needs a doctor. Do you understand or are you just too stupid to understand? The baby is sick."

"Si, señora, I understand."

Grace peered hard at the woman, staring her down. "I will return tomorrow, and when I do I want this place clean. I want clean diapers on those children. I want the food cleared from the table, and I want this terrible smell and the flies gone. Señor Tommy pays you to do a job. He will be very angry if I tell him what I found here today. Do I make myself clear?"

"Si, señora. Whatever you say, I will do."

Grace saw that the woman was clearly concerned.

This job was probably the only source of income for an entire family.

"Take care of these things by tomorrow. If you do as I say, you'll still have a position here; if you don't you will have to answer to me. Not to Señor Tommy, but to me." Then Grace stormed out of the house, carrying the baby to her car.

When she reached the car she was trembling and her face was wet with tears. She closed her eyes and prayed: "Forgive me Lord for losing my temper. I am weak, I was harsh with that woman. I am sorry Lord, but this baby is special. This is Felicita's baby....forgive me."

*　*　*

"Ten thousand dollars, Grace! That's our portion for an adoption. I mean the ministry's portion. It covers all the expenses—the medical, the foster care, and the birth-mother expenses. It doesn't include lawyers' fees. The families pay extra for that. We need this money, Grace. The mission needs the money."

Grace looked at her husband. Then she looked down

at the baby she was holding. "And the baby? Have you found a family for Felicita's baby?"

He shook his head. "No. Not yet. It's too soon. We don't have her paperwork."

"Were you inside that house? Have you seen how the babies are kept?"

Tommy didn't answer.

"It's inhumane. It's dangerous, Tommy. And it's certainly not the Christian thing to do. The babies could get sick, or even die in conditions like that."

"I'm sorry, Grace. I didn't realize. I'll check it out tomorrow. I promise."

"No, Tommy. I'll do it. I want to go back and see for myself. I told your worker she would have to answer to me."

He looked surprised, "Why?"

"Because these babies need me. Not just this baby, but all the babies. They need someone who cares. You say that the ministry needs this. Well, then, I want to help. This is something I can do. If you promise that these children truly need to be adopted, then I can assist and help keep them safe. Except…"

"Except…what? What's the catch?"

"Except, not this baby, not Felicita's baby."

"We can't place it for adoption?" He whined, clearly troubled by the request.

"I don't know."

"It's a lot of money. Elmer will not be pleased," Tommy warned, shaking his head. Grace could see in his face that he was upset, just short of angry. But then she thought of the babies in the squalid house and it didn't matter.

"I don't care if Elmer is pleased or not. And have you seen him lately? Is something wrong? He looks terrible. I think he might be ill. Besides, it's always the money with you. Why did you choose to work in a Christian ministry if money is so important? Was it just because your father started the mission? Why didn't you simply go into business? Or, maybe you have. Is that it Tommy? Have you gone into the adoption business? When did the mission start to do adoptions?"

He glared at her like a sulking child and didn't answer.

"I know Felicita, Tommy. She is my friend. What happens to her baby is my concern." She shifted the baby and looked at her face. "You and Elmer have other babies to place; unless, of course, they get sick and die or the authorities come knocking and take them away."

She watched her husband's face while he considered her words. Her fate and the baby's depended on how Tommy would react.

"Okay, you win," Tommy finally said, with resignation in his voice.

Grace sighed, and in her heart she said, *Thank you Lord.* She kissed the baby.

"What will you do with the baby?" he asked.

"I don't know," Grace said. "But one thing is certain. I'm not doing anything with Felicita's baby until I give the matter a lot of prayer. Something I would recommend for you also."

"I will," he replied, "in my own way. Just remember

to keep this business quiet. We don't want attention brought to the mission."

"The mission? You make me ashamed to be associated with the mission. You could go to jail for running a fattening house. You know it's illegal to buy babies."

"I'm not buying babies, Grace. I'm just helping poor women. That's all."

"And what would the authorities think of your help?"

Tommy said nothing. He just turned and walked away. *Every garden has a serpent,* Grace thought, *including mine.* She knew at that moment what she would and would not do with Felicita's baby. She would never place this baby for adoption, not with some foreign couple from Italy or England, or wherever—not even if they were rich and lived in the United States. She would keep this little girl, this precious gift. This would be her reward for all the selfish, inconsiderate things her husband had ever done. This treasure was payback for all she had lost and given up on her journey to today. She and her daughter would survive. More than survive, they would prosper in the little town of Canoguitas. They would live together in paradise....by the road with no name.

Jim Pahz

BREATHING BIRDLAND

My parents' marriage ended abruptly. It wasn't the kind of thing you saw coming. At least I didn't. Rather, it was more like dropping a vase, an irreplaceable family heirloom that fell to the floor and broke into a thousand pieces. It was there one minute and gone the next. My parents' marriage crashed in November, on Thanksgiving day.

The whole family was gathering at Mom and Dad's house for the holiday dinner. It was a typical November day in Michigan, grey and cold, and it looked like snow would fall any minute. The trees bent sideways, looking like they might topple over, but trying to get a foothold against the winds of winter that would inevitably come. Grandma Shirley was helping Mom with the turkey. My sister Elida was scheduled to come at 2:00 p.m. with her husband and three children.

We didn't notice when Dad left the house. It was probably ten or eleven in the morning. Apparently, he just walked out the door, got in his car, and drove off. It wasn't until one o'clock in the afternoon that Mom became aware of his absence. After Elida and her family arrived, we began speculating what could have happened to Dad. Mom decided to postpone our dinner, at least for an hour or so. By three o'clock the children were starting to complain they were hungry, so the family decided to serve the meal and save some food for Dad. Everyone expected he would be arriving at any time. We were wrong.

Dad didn't come back until the next day. By then Mom had notified the police department and called all the local hospitals. There hadn't been any news. When Dad returned he was quiet.

"Where were you?" my mother inquired. Her voice was concerned, but not overly alarmed or intimidating, just concerned.

"I didn't feel like celebrating," he said. Then, walking from the room, he headed up the stairs to the bedroom.

One look at my father and I knew something had changed. He was a different man. I didn't know what it was. At that time I didn't realize my parents' marriage was over, but I sensed something would never be the same. It was like one of those paradigm shifts I heard about in college. In subsequent weeks I came to realize my father's decision to forgo the Thanksgiving meal and later to abandon his family had to do with his breathing problems and in particular with those stupid pets.

* * *

Dad was a math professor and worked two days a week. On those days he worked four hours each day. He called those his "busy days" and it would be wrong to say he was over burdened with work. He had time to pursue other interests, if he had any. Unfortunately, Dad was frequently sick and didn't feel like doing much of anything. Mom and Dad lived in a house surrounded by twenty acres of woodland. Periodically, Dad became ill with a breathing disorder. At first it was diagnosed as chronic bronchitis, but later the doctors said it was asthma. Four or five times each year, Dad would be almost incapacitated. He would go to work with a pocket full of Jolly Ranchers or some other hard candy and pretend to be well enough to teach his class. I can't imagine what he must have been like in the classroom in that condition, I'm sure it wasn't pretty.

When he returned home, he would rub Vicks VapoRub on the bottoms of his feet, as well as his chest, and go to bed waiting for his cough to subside. When he exhaled, his chest sounded like an orchestra warming up before a recital. Sometimes it was like an old truck with a diesel engine. Once I told him he was purring like the leopard I saw on a television show about big cats in Africa. He didn't appreciate my observation.

When Dad was having his breathing problems, his noises would compete with the sound of the vaporizer. It ran continuously, hissing and spitting out water and steam, which hung in the air, mingling with the smell of Vicks. When his attacks got really bad, a doctor would prescribe antibiotics and Prednisone. In a week or so Dad would recover—until the next bout.

* * *

My Dad wasn't an animal lover. He hated cats. So it probably wasn't a good move for him when he acquiesced to my mother when she brought the first cat home. He explained he didn't want a cat, but somehow she persuaded him. Mom was a stubborn woman, and she really was an animal lover. Do opposites really attract? I don't know, but my parents were opposites. Mom promised it would be their only cat. The following month, when my father returned from a teaching conference, he found two more cats had arrived.

"They were Mrs. Grant's cats," Mom explained. Her voice had a pleading quality. "You remember, Gretchen. Well, Mr. Grant lost his job, and the family has to move to another city. They can't take the cats with them. If we don't take them they will have to go to the animal shelter and might be destroyed."

Dad objected, "That's Gretchen's problem, not ours." But eventually he gave in. Dad always gave in.

Mother promised they would be the last cats she ever brought home. Since they were older cats, she said, "They probably won't live much longer."

The dog arrived the following year. One of mom's colleagues from work brought it over. The woman explained how she wanted the dog to stay small, but it kept growing. Now it was too big for her grandson, who was only a toddler, and she was afraid it would accidentally knock the boy over. Mother fell in love with the dog immediately.

"We will call you Chance," Mom said, "because this will probably be your last chance to find a home."

Dad preferred dogs to cats, and Chance looked like Lassie. He had long golden hair and a noble appearance. So, although Dad wasn't enthusiastic about adopting a dog, he didn't put up much of a fuss.

As far as the second dog coming into our house, the blame must go to me. I had been reading the newspaper on a Sunday morning, and there was this story about a lady running a "puppy mill." She was raided by Animal Control and her hundred or so animals confiscated. It was a sad story. In addition to all the dogs, she had goats and farm animals wandering around the place. Most were starving and covered in filth. The officials actually found an unburied dead horse in the woman's backyard. The authorities were called after complaints from neighbors. The newspaper article concluded by saying if people didn't come forward and adopt the dogs and other animals, they would be euthanized. What could I do? I was a college freshman then and passionate about animal welfare. I convinced Dad to go to the animal shelter with me. Together we returned with a puppy. It was a little white thing with long hair. I named the dog Precious.

*　　*　　*

Three years ago Dad got bogged down in birds. He purchased his first peacocks in the springtime. He was at the fairgrounds with Erik, his five-year-old grandson. A man was selling peafowl, and Erik said, "Can we buy some, Grandpa?"

Dad could never refuse a request from a five-year-old, and Erik was a special child. When he returned home that afternoon, he had four baby chicks. Three years later there were nine adult peacocks. By then, Precious was grown. He had turned out to be a strange looking dog. He was about the size of a cocker spaniel, but with a lot more hair. You couldn't see his face at all, and since he was always chasing his tail, it was hard to know where he began or ended.

The year after the peacocks, Dad ordered thirty-five baby Guinea hens. He did this because he had read an article in *Mother Earth News* saying Guinea fowl consumed large quantities of ticks. Living in the country, as my parents did, there was a big population of deer. Dad was concerned because deer ticks carried Lyme Disease. He wanted to be "proactive." I remember that was the word he used. Dad always liked that word. He also liked "multitasking," and "pecksniffian."

"Let's get those ticks before they get us," Dad said. "We need to be proactive."

The peacocks and Guinea hens got along well together. They roamed free and at night roosted in the chicken house or tree tops. They made exotic bird sounds and in the summer it was like living in the jungle. Dad began to call the place Birdland. The only problem was you needed to park your car in the garage or the peacocks would walk all over it and leave scratch marks. Also, the peacocks liked to jump on people's vehicles and use them as a toilet.

And then the chickens came. That's what destroyed

the harmony of Birdland. Dad purchased baby chicks because he thought it would be good to get eggs. I don't know why, because Dad never ate eggs. But he did things like that, like the time he bought hunting land even though he had never hunted. Or when he decided he would have enjoyed a train set as a child and then spent a small fortune on a deluxe Lionel train layout. Round and round the train went, for about an hour, until Dad realized he was bored. He decided he really didn't want trains after all, so he boxed his locomotive and assorted boxcars and put them up in the garage. They are still there.

Dad's doctor had advised against eating eggs, as his cholesterol was high, but Dad wanted eggs. He bought the chicks last March and expected the chickens would roam free with the other birds. It didn't work out that way. Although they did produce eggs, when they roamed outside they tried to hide their nests. It was hard to find the eggs, and when you did, you weren't sure how long they had been there. Another problem was when the chickens free-ranged it was like they were on a mission to destroy Mom's vegetable garden and flowerbeds. They would scratch around looking for grubs and worms and tear up everything in their path.

One day, Dad decided he had enough of chickens. The refrigerator was filled with about twenty cartons of eggs. There wasn't room for much of anything else.

"I've had it with those foul creatures" he announced. "I don't even like eggs."

Dad went to K-mart and bought a BB gun, a Daisy Red Ryder. When Mom got wind of what Dad intended, she became enraged.

"You can't kill those chickens," she screamed.

"Why not?" Dad asked. "They're my chickens."

"No they're not. They're our chickens, and I can't allow it. They're not disposable like a Styrofoam cup. You can't just discard them because they're in the way."

"Sure I can." Dad began pouring BBs down the barrel of his Red Ryder.

"No, no." Mother was livid. "They're alive. They are imbued with the spirit of the Creator. Don't you want to be a good steward? You need to be green, to protect the earth and all its inhabitants."

"I'm not green. I don't care about the environment. I'll let you in on a secret, I'm not concerned with global warming, either. It doesn't matter to me if there is a hole in the ozone layer or what the size of my carbon footprint is. The only footprints I care about are those of the damn chickens and I'm going to erase those footprints." He began to cough. Dad reeked from the smell of menthol.

"You could just give the chickens away," Mom said.

"Too much trouble, it's easier just to shoot 'em. I want to shoot them."

"No, I'll take the chickens. I'll be the responsible person. You won't have to deal with them. But, I want them confined so they don't destroy my garden. There's poop everywhere. It's a frigging mine field out there. Help me catch them and lock them up and then you are through with them. Understand? You won't ever have to worry about chickens again."

So for the next hour or so, Mom and Dad captured all the birds and locked them in the chicken house. It was a struggle because some of the birds didn't want to be caged. They flapped their wings and dust flew everywhere. Three days later, Dad was sicker than ever.

When he recovered enough to get out of bed, he made an appointment with a pulmonologist. After the tests were run, the doctor had a conference with Mom and Dad.

"He had an asthma attack. He's sensitive. Do you have animals in the house?" The doctor asked.

"Yes—three cats and two dogs."

"You probably should get rid of them."

Mom objected. "Why? He's had animals in the house for thirty years. He's been fine. Okay, sometimes he gets sick, but he never had an attack as bad as the last one. It was the birds. He went into the chicken house and breathed in the dust. Last year when he went into the bird house he also got sick… only not as bad."

"Asthma," the doctor repeated. "He's sensitive to foreign particles. Cats and dogs have dander. He shouldn't be exposed to animals. It's not good for him. The smaller the quantity of particulate matter he is exposed to, the better."

*   *   *

I always found it interesting how two people can hear the same thing, but come away with two different messages. When Mom and Dad returned home from the doctor's, I was sitting in the kitchen. They were discussing pets. I heard Mom say:

"The inside animals have been there for years, and you shouldn't be concerned about them. They're not the problem. Your illness," she continued, "is entirely because you breathed the dust in the chicken coop. You need to stay out of there."

"But the doctor said we should get rid of the pets we keep in the house."

"No, dear, that's not what he said. The doctor said you need to reduce your exposure to things that can be harmful—like dust or grass clippings or perfume or the smell of cleaning fluid. You have allergies. Remember when you were tested eight years ago for allergies? What did the allergist say? He said you were allergic to ragweed and grass clippings. He didn't say anything about dogs or cats. In fact, when he did that skin test on your back, dogs and cats tested negative. So what does that test tell you? It tells you that when you cut the lawn you will need to be careful. Probably you should wear a face mask."

"If the situation was reversed," Dad said, "if the Doctor asked me to get rid of the cats, I know what I would do. Without a moment's hesitation, they'd be gone."

"You only say that because you hate cats."

"I'm not fond of cats, especially in the house. I admit it, but that doesn't change things. Even if I loved cats, I'd get rid of them because I love you more than I could love animals. People are more important." Dad hung his head.

Mother was unmoved. "I'm sorry," she said. "I don't believe you. You're trying to manipulate me. That's what you do. Stop pouting. The pets in the house stay—they're part of our family."

And that was that. Like two prize fighters they moved to their respective corners and didn't discuss the matter further.

*   *   *

The incident on Thanksgiving became known in our family as Black Friday. It had nothing to do with shopping. Years later, my mom would refer to it as "the year your father became the turkey."

After Dad returned home on Black Friday, he didn't talk about why he had disappeared or where he had gone. His lack of communication frustrated everyone in the family. But, Mom needed answers. She must have felt she was entitled to know why he left or maybe she felt she was losing control of the situation. Mom went into her three stages of confrontation. Stage one was debate mode. She appealed to Dad's reason.

"Don't you realize how rude your behavior was, how inconsiderate and selfish? Are you aware you completely ruined Thanksgiving dinner for the rest of us? Your self-absorption," Mom pointed out, "is indicative of an overly developed id. You are nothing more than a big baby. Your behavior was tantamount to throwing an emotional temper tantrum. What do you have to say for yourself? I think you owe us all an explanation. Well, are you going to apologize?"

Dad didn't apologize. He ignored her, acting like she wasn't even in the room. He picked up a magazine and began to read it.

Having failed with the first approach, Mom went into stage two—fighting mode. She became aggressive, like a Siamese fighting fish in a glass bowl. She hurled epithets at him and demonstrated an impressive proficiency in the use of profanity.

"You're a big fuck-head," she screamed. That was over the top for Mom. She hardly ever used the F-word. For emphasis, she hurled a dish against the wall. It shattered.

Dad hardly noticed. He went on reading his magazine as if Mother wasn't even in the room. Poor Mom had no choice but to go into stage three, which was usually reserved for extreme emergencies. She became emotional. She wept like a willow, shifting gears as smoothly as if she had been driving for NASCAR. One minute she was Attila the Hun, the next poor, pitiful mom, flailing about like the fighting fish out of its bowl.

"Okay, maybe it's my fault. But I'm not a mind

reader. Maybe you wanted sweet potatoes instead of mashed potatoes. How was I to know? I can't read your mind. You could have said something. You're breaking my heart. I'm in distress, and you don't seem to be concerned. Do you care?"

If he did, he didn't show it. He remained impassive, aloof to the storm that raged around him. Finally, he put his magazine down and turned to Mom.

"Do we have potato chips?" he asked. "I'm hungry."

* * *

Dad never told anyone the day he bought his condominium. It was his secret act of defiance, his final statement on the subject. I guess he figured there was no point to arguing anymore. Thanksgiving had come and gone. Mother probably wasn't going to change her mind about the inside pets. She prided herself on her stubbornness—which she referred to as being steadfast and resolute.

After Thanksgiving, Dad began moving around like a man in a fog. He seemed preoccupied. He wouldn't answer questions, except to say yes, or no. He didn't make polite conversation or chitchat. He seemed to lose interest in everything. On the days he went to work—his busy days— he fed himself breakfast, filled his pockets with hard candies, and slipped quietly from the house. Eventually, this became his routine.

Then, one day in February, Dad didn't return home. It took us two days to learn he had moved into his new condominium.

We were surprised, and Mom was furious. When she finally caught up with him, she demanded an explanation and said she was entitled to one.

He merely shrugged his shoulders and said, "It's simple. I know what you're doing. You're trying to kill me. Now I'm safe. My condo is my fort. Besides, there's no carpet there. I have laminate flooring that's easy to keep clean. I can breathe better. The air is pure, and I'm not always wheezing. Best of all, there are no pets, the blood-suckers are gone."

A few days later Mom was served with a petition for divorce. The papers stipulated the cause as irreconcilable differences. The two settled amicably.

*　*　*

My parents went on with their lives—although separately. Dad continued to teach at the university. I didn't see him as much as I used to, but when I did, he didn't cough or wheeze. He started to dress better, and he no longer smelled like menthol. He settled nicely into single life and subscribed to a computer dating service.

Mom retired from her job at the library. She didn't speak much about Dad, except when talking about raising birds. Then she would refer to him as the only turkey she ever had at Birdland. "It was harder to live with that turkey," she said, "than all the peacocks, guineas, or chickens combined." But, really, Mom didn't speak much about Dad or the divorce. She wasn't at peace with the subject. But she wasn't the kind of person to dwell on the past. Besides, she had her chores to do. There were the birds to attend to and the eggs to gather. With two dogs and three cats, she was a busy woman.

One day a neighbor brought over a kitten that needed a home. She asked Mom if there was room for one more pet?

"Of course there is," Mom said. "Look at that face. How adorable. How can we refuse such a beautiful kitty?"

BAD HAIR DAY*

From the time my brother was a toddler my family always called him Mikey. The name seemed to fit him. Mikey was a rascal who loved dressing up in costumes and wearing hats. But that was a long time ago, and now as a grown man he objected to his name. He wanted to be called Mick. He said Mikey was childish and unsophisticated. The name Mick was more in keeping with his appearance, which was impeccable. Whoever he was, he was always immaculately dressed and looked like he just stepped off the pages of a gentleman's fashion magazine. My brother liked clothes more than any man I ever met. You could say he was obsessed with his appearance. He wore the most fashionable brands of apparel and always carried an attaché case.

Now married, Mikey and his new wife, Kelly, had amassed all the trappings of the good life, including a new house in the suburbs and two luxury automobiles. My brother worked as a buyer for Saks Fifth Avenue.

I hadn't seen him in some time, about six years. I had gone to college, served in the military and was living on the west coast. I was teaching at a high school and returned to Long Island for a Christmas visit with my family and looking forward to seeing my brother again and to meeting his new wife.

We hadn't parted under the best of circumstances. My brother liked to tease. His idea of a good time was to ridicule or berate someone until he made them show signs of discomfort. The more miserable they became the better. He went for the jugular every time. With my younger sister he would focus on her weight. My sister always was slightly chubby but never what you would call fat. However, when she was a teenager she was very sensitive and he would chide her: "You're fat," imitating Ed Norton from the Jackie Gleason reruns we used to watch on television. If she was going out somewhere like the movies he would say: "You better take extra money with you, I hear they're basing the ticket prices on weight. They're charging by the pound." This would immediately cause a reaction from my sister and usually resulted in a torrent of tears. Then she would scream at him about how mean he was. That would make him laugh.

I had several vulnerable points my brother could attack. But what he liked best to make fun of was my clothes. He did this throughout high school and I only escaped his taunting when I went off to college. I didn't cry or scream as my sister did, but I was glad when the opportunity came and I could finally escape. Now, after an absence of six years, we sat down to the dinner table. I could see right away that my brother couldn't wait to pick up where he had left off.

"Where do you buy your clothes," he said while appraising me from head to foot, "from K-Mart?" My brother smirked. "Is that the Martha Stewart or Jaclyn Smith collection? How much did that sweater cost?"

"I don't know," I replied. I had never been concerned with my wardrobe. "What's wrong with my sweater anyway?"

Mikey waved his hands. "Nothing. Nothing's wrong with the sweater or your blue jeans either. They're lovely.

What is your sweater made of anyway—polyester?"

I wasn't sure what Mikey meant, but I suspected it wasn't a compliment.

"What kind of person cares so much about clothing anyway?" I asked. "If it doesn't itch I'm happy with it. Surely there are more important things than apparel."

"No," Mikey said. "There isn't! Haven't you heard that clothes make the man?"

"I never believed that," I said, "it's silly."

"Now, boys," Kelly interrupted. "No arguing at the dinner table. Remember you are brothers and you haven't seen each other for a long time. You should be nice. I cooked too hard all day to have dinner ruined."

"It looks delicious, baby," Mikey said, offering a condescending smile and taking a bite of his salad. "She's a great cook, isn't she, Daniel?"

"Yes she is," I agreed. I was glad to see my brother change his focus to the food. "This is a terrific meal."

Kelly had made a Caesar salad, and cooked t-bone steaks and twice-baked potatoes. A chocolate mousse was on the menu for desert. The table was beautifully set with their wedding china and a white tablecloth. Candles were lit and Christmas music played softly in the background. It was an opportunity for my brother to show off the lifestyle he was so proud of. I couldn't help admiring him.

"And she's good looking, too, isn't she?" Mikey inquired. "You have to admit she's a good-looking woman. You should see how she looks in fish-net stockings."

I could imagine. "Yes she is," I answered. Although in agreement, I felt uncomfortable. It seemed an inappropriate thing for my brother to say. "I can see you're a lucky man, Mikey."

Kelly smiled and thanked me. Even in the candlelight I could see she was flushed and embarrassed.

"It's Mick, not Mikey," my brother snapped. He glared at me and I could see he was serious about this name thing.

"Mick... Mikey, what's the difference? A rose by any other name, and all of that stuff. What's in a name, anyway? By the way, Mick, do you still have your ears?"

"Ears?" Kelly asked. "What ears?"

Mikey leaned back in his seat and looked annoyed.

"Go ahead, tell her," I said. "She'll like the story."

But Mikey remained silent. He tried to yawn, feigning indifference. Kelly prodded him: "Come on," she pleaded. "This isn't fair. Will someone please tell me about the ears?"

I could see Mikey wasn't planning to say anything so I continued: "When Mikey was a kid he always liked hats. He liked to play dress-up. Anyway, for his fifth birthday he joined the Mickey Mouse Club and got a set of ears. You know, one of those Mouseketeer hats with the big mouse ears? He loved that hat so much. He wore it everywhere. I think he even slept with it on his head at night."

"Oh honey," Kelly cooed. "That's so sweet!" She got up and stood behind her husband's chair. "I'll bet you looked so cute," she said, kissing the top of his head.

"I jog five miles every day," Mikey said. Apparently he had heard enough about his mouse ears. He was changing the subject. "You know Daniel, you have to look good to feel good."

"Okay," I said, "do you feel good?"

"Yes, I do. I feel great. Don't you have any pride in your appearance? Where do you buy your ties from?"

"I don't wear ties. I can't remember when the last time was that I wore a tie. Whenever I wear one I feel like I'm being strangled. But if I did buy ties, I think I would buy them wherever I could get the best price. I'm a teacher, remember? Teachers don't make fashion statements, they have more important things to do."

"Well," Mikey said, "I guess there is nothing wrong with buying your ties from a discount store. Discount stores have their place. But have you considered how really bad you look? I mean you look terrible. You have no sense of fashion whatsoever."

Back and forth our conversation over my apparel limped, like a wounded bird tormented by a cat. The bird suffering numerous blows until finally exhausted, it dropped and died in the middle of the dining room table about the time the chocolate mouse was finished. My brother and I got up and moved like two professional fighters to our respective corners. But instead of corners we went into the living room to watch some television while Kelly cleaned up the table. In about thirty minutes Mikey fell asleep on his back and began to snore. It was 9:45 p.m. Kelly apologized to me and then went and gently woke her husband. She explained that Mick had a long commute in the morning to Manhattan and because of traffic had to leave the house by 5:30 a.m. After checking the doors and turning everything off downstairs, we said goodnight and retired upstairs to our respective bedrooms.

I was awakened from sleep by loud voices drifting through the walls. I sat up in bed, and remembered that Mikey had to get up early. I looked at the clock radio on the night table; it said 4:45 a.m. I fell back into bed and pulled up the covers. The noise outside the room continued, so I began to listen. I wondered what the problem was. Again I sat up, straining to decipher the words coming from the other room. Mikey was yelling something. Curious, I got out of bed and crept toward the door. I leaned my ear against the wall and heard Kelly's voice now, low and calm. Then I heard Mikey, loud and accusatory. They were having a fight. Apparently they forgot, or didn't care, that there was a guest in the house. Maybe they thought I was still asleep and didn't hear them.

"God damn it!" Mikey yelled. "The collar's not right. It doesn't fit."

"I'm sorry," Kelly whined. "I worked all night on it. If it doesn't fit, I'll fix it later."

"I need it *today*, damn it! I'm going to the Rotary Club. I've got a sales presentation to make. I need it now!"

"Now?" Kelly was sounding hysterical. "I can't fix it now. The stitches have to come out." There was calm for close to a minute, and I imagined Mikey frantically searching the closet for a different shirt.

The silence was broken again by my brother. "Shit," he yelled. "Where's the goddamn hair dryer?" Muffled noise, then a desperate announcement to the universe: "I can't find the fucking hair dryer!"

"Wait…Mick." Kelly's voice had a frantic quality. "I

left the dryer at your mother's house."

This admission elicited an explosion of epithets. "You what? You did what? You left the hair dryer at Mother's? Goddamn it! What am I supposed to do? What about my hair?" I imagined a volcano erupting with sparks flying and lava flowing.

"Selfish bitch! Do you know how selfish you are?"

"I'm sorry," Kelly was crying now. "I'm not selfish. I just made a mistake. How can you call me selfish when you know I stayed up all night working on your shirt?"

"Yeah… you did a fine job on the shirt, didn't you? A great fucking job. What's the first thing you did this morning when you got up?"

There was a pause. "Well, Kelly"—he drew her name out slowly—"the first thing you did when you got up was go to the bathroom. You know I need the bathroom to get ready for work. My appearance is important—it's what pays the bills. So, you're pretty selfish, if you ask me."

"Mikey!" Kelly screamed. "I had to go to the bathroom, that's all. I had to pee and take my pill. My God, that can't be bad. You sound crazy! You know that? You sound like a crazy person."

She shouldn't have called him crazy, even if it was true. As expected, when my brother next spoke he sounded infuriated.

"Fuck you!" He hurled the insult at her as if he were Zeus throwing a thunderbolt.

He has gotten mean, I thought as I backed away from the door.

"Fuck you, too!" Kelly screamed back.

Good for her I thought, rooting for Kelly.

A door slammed and when I heard Kelly's voice again, it was muffled. She probably was in the bathroom. "Do your own fucking hair. I'm not doing it any more." She yelled: "I'm finished doing your hair!"

This threat was followed by a pause. Then, in a much calmer voice, Mikey began to plead with Kelly to open the door.

He said: "Come on honey. Open the door. I'm sorry I overreacted. It's just that this presentation is important. I've got a lot of pressure, that's all. You understand. No one can do my hair like you can. I need you to help me with my hair, baby." His voice was consoling and gentle. "We can use your hot comb. I'm sorry I said you were selfish, I know you work hard. But no one is perfect. It was a mistake, that's all. You shouldn't have left my hair dryer at Mom's. That was kind of thoughtless, you know."

This calmer, more rational man succeeded in convincing Kelly to open the bathroom door, but he had failed to calm her down. She was truly hysterical now, both crying and shouting at the top of her voice, "All right. All right. I'm selfish and I'm stupid. I left your goddamn hair dryer at your mom's. Why can't you just get a second hair dryer—one for your mother's house and one for here? But, no... that's too easy. It's much better if I'm responsible for remembering your hair dryer as well as everything else around here. I do the housework, the cooking, entertain your relatives, and make you custom shirts. Do you even care how much I work? I can do a hundred things right and you never notice; but God forbid, I make one mistake and you come all unglued. Like you never make a mistake! All you really care about is your stupid hair and your goddamn shirts and your new suits and... Hell, I can't even piss in the morning!"

"All right, I'm sorry, Kelly. Listen, I'm going to be late for work if you don't do my hair soon. I'm really sorry I got so angry. But remember, Kelly, I do it all for you. Have I ever missed a paycheck? So *please* Kelly, do my hair before I'm late? We'll pick up a second hair dryer later. Okay honey?"

It was quiet after that. Apparently, the fight was over, but I stood transfixed by the door. After a few minutes I opened my door, just a crack, to peek out. I saw my brother emerge from his room and go into the hall. He wore a black suit, with a white shirt and red tie. I watched as Mikey stood facing the hall mirror and straightened his tie. Then, apparently satisfied with his appearance, he smoothed his hair, picked up his attaché case and descended the stairs.

My brother looked good. I have to admit that. He looked successful. *Maybe clothes do make the man.* In any event, he didn't look like my kid brother Mikey. He looked like… like Mick.

LIFE WITHOUT DUMPLINGS

"You're a curmudgeon. You know that? You're excessively short-tempered and grouchy."

Robert couldn't help it. He had withdrawn into himself like a telescope. He did this when he was depressed or angry. This was one of those times and he was sure it was his wife Carol's fault. She was supposed to be waiting for him in front of the rest room. The Cracker Barrel was busy so they had put their name on the waiting list. After driving for hours, Robert was looking forward to a meal of chicken and dumplings. But when Robert came out of the bathroom, Carol was nowhere to be seen. Maybe she's in the restroom, he thought. So he waited, but she never emerged. After five minutes he thought he better look in the dining room. It was a huge room divided into sections. He passed through the first section, and all the tables were filled. He didn't see Carol anywhere. He was starting to panic. He walked into the second section and was looking around. Again the room was full, but finally he saw Carol sitting alone at a table toward the back of the room. Robert approached her.

"You abandoned me," he stammered. "How could you do that?"

"Don't be silly. They called our name, and I wanted to get the table. Otherwise we would have missed it, and we would have to go to the bottom of the list. You must have heard the announcement over the loud speakers. I know you can hear those things in the bathroom. I assumed you would come looking for me."

Robert had not heard them call his name. These days he wasn't hearing much of anything. He had been retired five years, and he and Carol were returning from a trip to their daughter's house in Pennsylvania. Since Patty's divorce she had remained single and moved from Ohio to find a better job. Robert missed his grandchildren a great deal.

Now he was angry. He could barely contain himself. He sat with his head hung low, feeling sorry for himself. He was giving Carol the silent treatment.

"I wish you wouldn't be so temperamental," Carol

said. "It doesn't become you. You're better than that."

*   *   *

A long time ago, after graduating college, Robert took a year off to find himself. The thought of going to work worried him. Carol suggested he return to school for an advanced degree, which would postpone him from entering the labor force. She pointed out that continuing his education would be an acceptable alternative to everyone—especially their parents.

"People appreciate a scholar," Carol said.

"But what will I study?" Robert asked.

"We can go to the library and look through catalogues and find something."

So the two of them leafed through the bulletins of several American universities and settled on one in Indiana. Carol suggested he major in Health Education.

"What is Health Education?" he asked Carol.

"I'm not sure, but I think it has something to do with health. I think you could do it."

"I thought doctors and nurses did that sort of thing."

"Maybe, I don't know," Carol replied. "If you prefer you could study astrophysics. It's all right with me. I was just making a suggestion."

Robert and Carol moved to Indiana and he entered graduate school to become a Health Educator. In a few years he had earned a master's and doctoral degree. Eventually he had to leave school to earn a living. Since he couldn't do much of anything, he applied for a teaching position. He sent out fifty-seven resumes and had two job offers. He accepted a position at a small college in Ohio.

When Robert first met his department chairperson, a large, red cheeked woman with sagging jowls, she reminded him of a bulldog.

"What do you know of drugs?" she barked.

"Not much," Robert answered. "They're not good for you. There's a war on drugs. I guess I know as much as the next person. Just say no."

"Yes, yes" the chairperson said, "You're going to need more than a few platitudes, so you'd better learn. School starts next week. I suggest you go to the library and become an expert. Student evaluations are important at this university."

So Robert began his first assignment by teaching a course entitled *Drug Dependency and Abuse,* and another course named, *Alcohol Problems.* These were subjects he learned something about the previous week while cramming in the library and developing his expertise. He had never studied about drugs in college, and he had little personal experience.

*   *   *

When Robert began teaching he was nervous. He was not accustomed to standing in front of a group of people. The first time he addressed his students he perspired profusely and could hardly speak. He was convinced his students knew more on the topic than he did. He wasn't much of a drinker and he had never smoked marijuana. He found it hard to be an authority on a topic with which he was so ill suited.

It wasn't that Robert was merely at a loss for words, he literally couldn't speak. It felt like he had something stuck in his throat that was choking him. When he tried to talk, he made gurgled, unintelligible noises. The students laughed as he stood clutching and massaging his neck looking as if he was trying to remove an arrow.

Robert went to the doctor and explained his predicament.

"It feels like I have something in my throat like an orange." Robert pointed to his neck.

"You mean your Adam's Orange?" The doctor grinned.

"It's not funny," Robert said. "I can't do my job. It's bad enough my students are making fun of me."

"Of course it's not funny." The doctor adopted a more sober attitude. He examined Robert's throat and ran his finger down Robert's neck and said, "You feel that notch? That is your cricoids cartilage. It is the last cartilage of your larynx. What you are experiencing is a cricopharyngeal spasm."

"So, there is something wrong with my neck?"

"Not really. What you feel is caused by anxiety. It's a manifestation of an emotional problem. Is something bothering you?"

"Teaching," Robert confessed. He explained he had recently started his career and when he looked out at the hundred or so faces in the classroom it was disconcerting. "Sometimes the room spins and I perspire a lot."

"You might try and find a new job," the doctor advised. He smiled again. "Or, maybe you could learn to relax. In the meantime I will prescribe something to help you calm down."

So a calmer, drug-supported Robert practiced delivering lectures in front of Carol. He was more relaxed now. In his next few attempts in the classroom his teaching improved, although he was lethargic and prone to slurring his words. Over time he became a better, more confident instructor and gradually managed to wean himself off his medication.

*   *   *

Robert came to believe the goal of education was not that students actually learned anything, but rather that they *thought* they were learning. Robert believed it was his job to create the illusion of learning, like a magician pulling a rabbit from a hat. If he really tried to teach, Robert knew his student evaluations would be poor. At Robert's school a great deal of importance was placed on evaluations. His bulldog chairperson was right in that regard. Evaluations determined if Robert would get tenure or be promoted. Therefore, Robert taught with the goal to keep the students satisfied. Happy students meant good evaluations. To accomplish this he tried to entertain his students. He told jokes and stories. Some of the tales were true, but most of them he made up. Occasionally he brought pizza or some other treat to class. He learned the more food he offered during a semester the happier the students, thus, higher scores on his evaluations. Robert wanted his students to like him. He didn't want to cause stress or have too high expectations placed on them. He was more than a teacher, he was their friend.

Although Robert was quite sure he had figured out the system, he didn't expect to remain in education permanently. Teaching wasn't a good fit, and yet, there didn't seem to be anything for which he was better suited, even though he had extracted the imaginary arrow from is neck.

Professionally speaking, Robert didn't cast much of a shadow. Inconspicuous by design, he tried to avoid his department chairperson as well as the dean of his college. He went about his business quietly and unobtrusively.

One of his colleagues had a wooden plaque on his wall which read:

Do nothing

Say nothing

Be nothing

Humph... what nonsense. I prefer to be invisible. The sign should say; do nothing, say nothing, and you won't get in trouble. Robert didn't want to set the world on fire, he just wanted to keep from getting burned. So when newspaper reporters called for an opinion on drugs, Robert would refer the reporter to the bulldog or somebody else—anybody else. When a request would come for Robert to complete a survey, he would reply, "I'm sorry, I'm too busy to do surveys. My students come first."

Robert didn't pursue his career like a thoroughbred racehorse in training, but more like a draft animal with slow but steady effort. His rules—do the minimum, never volunteer, avoid committee work. He thought of putting his rules on a sign but worried it might not be politically correct. Besides, his colleagues would start referring to him as "dead wood," a derogatory term used in academia. Robert knew he was about as woodified as Pinocchio, but it was his secret. So Robert kept up appearances. He bothered nobody and he never garnered complaints from students or faculty. He was prompt for class, always in his office when he was supposed to be, and pleasant to colleagues and students. These things were all the university really wanted, even though the school administration was constantly clamoring for research, publications, and improved student evaluations. As long as nobody complained about Robert he was safe.

Robert didn't mind teaching—exactly. Sometimes he even enjoyed it and had some interesting experiences in the classroom. Like the time a student approached him after class asking, "Professor, when will we put on the tourniquets?"

"What?" Robert asked. He didn't understand what the student was talking about. He was having what his students referred to as a *brain fart*—he had gone totally blank. "I'm sorry," Robert said, "I don't understand your meaning."

"You know, dude, like when a man breaks his arm and you need to help him by putting his arm in one of those things."

Dude? Robert didn't see himself as a dude. He was a professor and scholar, a learned man.

"What course do you think you're taking?" Robert inquired.

"First aid. Isn't this first aid?"

"No. This is *Drug Dependency and Abuse.* We are in the fifth week of the semester. You've been here for five weeks, fifteen class periods, and don't know which course you're in?"

"Oops...' my bad?" The student grinned like a Cheshire cat and shuffled from the classroom. Robert never saw that student again.

One day in class Robert was talking about hobbies. He was trying to make the point that there were constructive as well as destructive ways to achieve excitement, drug abuse being a destructive way.

"How many of you have hobbies?" Robert asked. "And what are they?"

The responses were the usual: stamp collecting, jogging, listening to music, blah, blah, blah. It was boring. How many times had Robert asked this stupid question?

He noticed a young woman at the back of the room with her hand raised.

Robert called on her. "Yes, young lady, do you collect anything?"

"Road kill," she said.

"What?" Robert thought he either heard her wrong or she was intentionally misleading him. All of the students stopped their usual fidgeting and stared at the young woman.

"All right," he said, "I'll bite. Would you like to tell us something about your hobby?"

"Well, Professor, it's like this. I keep an aluminum scoop shovel in my trunk. When I see an animal that is in good condition, I scrape it up and bring it home. In my basement I have a stainless steel tank that contains flesh-eating beetles. The bugs are always hungry and after a few days there is nothing left except bones. I wash the bones and then reassemble them like a child might build a model airplane."

"I see," Robert said. "That's an interesting hobby." He wondered if the sarcasm in his voice came through. Apparently it did because she said nothing else.

When it came time to do oral presentations, about six weeks later, the girl brought in skeletons of a cat, a raccoon, and an opossum.

"I could tell you didn't believe me, professor," she said. "So, I offer this as proof. I assembled these skeletons from animals I picked up from the road."

"An unusual hobby," Robert said. He was at a loss for words.

*   *   *

Through the years Robert had other interesting class experiences, but mostly they were bland and predictable. The students always said more or less the same things.

Sometimes he would ask them to anonymously make a searching and moral inventory of things they had done which they now regretted or felt ashamed of. He was illustrating a step from Alcoholics Anonymous. "Before you can change your behavior," Robert said, "you must first acknowledge what you have done." Robert always hoped he would get something salacious or juicy, at least something interesting. But no, all he got were the same old responses: "I slept with my best friend's boyfriend; I stole money from Mom's purse; I cheated on Mrs. Melville's final exam." Robert thought these transgressions hardly worth the ink used to write them on paper. It was like seeing a bad movie for the fiftieth time.

Although remaining longer in his chosen profession than he originally intended, Robert continued to regard teaching as a temporary job. He always held out the hope for something more, but he hadn't the slightest idea of what that would be. In the meantime, teaching was a way to earn a paycheck. He still wanted to avoid a nine-to-five schedule. Academia afforded him that and also presented him with some nice perks. What Robert valued was family and free time to devote to other activities, like fishing with his grandchildren. When Robert was on campus performing his duties he functioned mostly on automatic pilot. He watched the clock and looked forward each day to leaving school.

The problem, as Robert saw it, was he was aging while the students were staying the same. They were always nineteen years old, but each year he was a year older. It became increasingly difficult to relate to them as people. Robert noticed that since the advent of computers the writing ability of his students declined. Now they wrote compositions as one would write a text message. They abbreviated words and made grammatical errors like using a small i when they should use a capital I, or writing code words like LOL for *laughing out loud*. At the same time he noticed that students had a greater sense of entitlement, expecting better grades for less and substantially poorer work. Many of his students disfigured themselves by covering their bodies with tattoos or wearing face piercings. Robert found both practices abhorrent. His students all carried cell phones and would sit in class texting. Robert was at a loss to understand this younger generation and eventually he stopped trying. As Robert grew older he was less and less concerned about being their friend. He just wanted to do his job and go home.

Semester after semester Robert plodded along. Each morning he would face his wife and say, "I'm not looking forward to teaching today." Then off he would go.

*　*　*

What made Robert most aware of the passage of time was the development of his hearing loss. He first noticed it when he had to ask students to repeat themselves. Their words sounded garbled and indistinct. Robert would hear only part of a sentence and then he would extrapolate or assume what the remainder was. Usually this worked, but sometimes it led to strange conversations. For example, the time a student remarked, "My mother beat her cancer."

But Robert heard, "My mother beat her hamster."

"Why would anyone hurt a hamster? Was it her pet?"

"No Professor, not her hamster, her cancer. My

mother is a cancer survivor." The students laughed.

"Oh," said Robert. "I'm glad to hear that. I hope she recovers."

Then there was the time Robert was talking to his grandson, David. The child was eight years old and had become upset because he had heard his father accuse his mother of having an affair.

One day the little boy asked, "Grandpa, what is an affair?"

Robert didn't hear him well but answered, "It's when your classmates from school get together to share their science projects."

The little boy looked bewildered. "Thank you Grandpa," he said, and walked away.

It took three days before Robert figured out his grandson wasn't talking about a science fair. Robert decided then he should have his hearing checked.

*　*　*

"Presbycusis," was the term the audiologist used. "Age related hearing loss. A hearing aid might help." But

Robert didn't want to wear a device in his ear. He said it would make him look like a space man or one of his students who came to class with a telephone sprouting from their ear. He thought the device was called blue teeth or something equally stupid. The episode with the audiologist was proof he was aging, as was his expanding waist size. Robert couldn't deny it. He wasn't a kid anymore and it was unlikely he would someday have a different occupation; a career in space or being employed as a white hunter in Africa were no longer options. Robert began to think in terms of retirement and when he would be eligible to draw social security benefits. That was seven years ago.

*   *   *

And now Robert sat in a Cracker Barrel Restaurant, somewhere between Philadelphia and Cleveland.

"Can I take your order?" the waitress said.

Carol placed her order, and then Robert said he wanted chicken and dumplings.

"I'm sorry," the waitress replied. "We just ran out of dumplings. We will have more in about thirty minutes."

No dumplings? This was the cruelest cut. It was worse than being abandoned by Carol while he was in the restroom. For the last hundred miles he had been driving through Pennsylvania looking for a Cracker Barrel Restaurant so he could get his chicken and dumplings. And now the restaurant was out of them. At this moment, in this place, the only thing in the world that would appease Robert was a plate of chicken and dumplings.

"I came especially for the dumplings," Robert whined. "Why don't you have dumplings?"

"I'm sorry sir. We're busy. We ran out. It's only temporary. If you are willing to wait we will have more in half an hour."

"No. I'm not willing to wait. I have an appointment. Just bring me a bowl of soup—chicken soup or minestrone. I don't care. You're not out of soup are you?"

As soon as the waitress left, Robert indicated he was going to leave. "They've lost my business," he said. "I'm going to another restaurant and I'm never coming back here." He got to his feet.

"Robert, sit down. You're not a baby. The reality is, you don't always get dumplings. That's life. But if you want them so much we can wait. I'm not eating alone, and I'm not leaving. Neither are you. We already placed our order and we are going to wait until our food comes. Do you understand? You're having a moment, Robert, a moment."

Robert sat down. He pursed his lips and sulked. He put his head between both hands and starred down at the table like he was in deep contemplation.

"Having a moment," he mumbled in a mocking tone. "You sound like one of my former students." He paused, and then he looked at his wife. "You know," he said, "this is a disastrous culinary experience."

"Yes dear, I know, but sometimes these things happen. You'll survive. I'm counting on you to be strong and not to be rude."

"Okay," Robert replied. He was feeling a little better now. Probably it was because he didn't hear his wife clearly and the words ran together and sounded garbled. He thought she said: "Yes dear, I was wrong. I'll drive for a while. Okay, dude?"

Robert smiled. When was the last time someone called him a dude? It was back in school, several years ago when Robert was still in the classroom. He reflected for a moment and then his smile broadened. He thought of his former career and all the students that had passed his way. Those were good times, he thought. *I miss it.* He wondered if he were still in the classroom, what he would be doing now to get ready for class.

Jim Pahz

DON'T POKE THE BEAR

It had been a long day and I was tired. The meeting at the foundation had taken longer than anticipated. The Board voted to raise the stipend adoptive families would receive to help defray expenses. I supported the motion because the cost to adopt internationally was growing higher all the time. But because the meeting lasted longer than expected, I had to miss another scheduled appointment with the Builders' Association.

I was asking myself how many projects I could keep juggling in the air when I turned the Lexus off the road and onto my driveway. Spring was morphing into early summer, and as I drove through the iron gates by the first pond, I slowed my speed to catch a glimpse of a koi. The colorful fish always raised my spirits. I drove by the man-made mountain with the waterfall meandering down the rocks and over a ten-foot drop. As the driveway divided and began the teardrop-shaped circle, I reached the second pond, and that was when I first noticed the red car about an eighth of a mile ahead parked in front of my house.

When I came to the vehicle I was surprised by how ugly it was. The automobile was a bomb—a real jalopy. The front bumper hung so precariously uneven that it looked about to fall off. One side of the car had a red door, but the door behind it was green. Several patches of rust indicated the car was ancient. I wondered *who would drive such a car?* Then my emotion changed from curiosity to annoyance. I didn't really care whose car it was; it didn't belong in front of my house. One of the reasons for having a house sitting at the back of thirty-five secluded acres was privacy. There was a sign on one of the pillars by the driveway that said *Keep Out, Private Property.* That sign wasn't a joke; I meant those words. I was quite sure whoever owned this car hadn't been invited, which meant they were either casing the property or trying to sell something. Either way, I was angry. Somebody was violating my space and my right to peace and tranquility.

Then I saw a man sitting on my front porch in my

wooden rocking chair with a silly grin on his face like that cat from Disney's *Alice in Wonderland*—the cat with the big teeth.

"I beg your pardon," I snapped as I got out of my car. "Can I help you?"

He didn't say anything. He just kept smiling and took a puff on his cigarette. I noticed he held a cardboard box in his lap. It looked like an old shoe box. Everything about him made me uneasy, so I made a fast assessment, looking him over from top to bottom. He wasn't familiar. He was overweight, puffy, with a stubble of a beard. His grayish brown hair appeared long and greasy and stuck out in every direction from beneath a stained baseball cap. I doubted if the man had washed his hair in a month and remember thinking *this is the kind of loser who would drive a hunk of junk like the one parked in my driveway.* Then I thought of Gretchen. Was she safe? Where was she? I remembered it was her turn to volunteer at the country club and my momentary panic for my wife's welfare dissipated. I looked around to see if others were present—no one except for this sad loser in my rocking chair with a shoebox on his lap.

*   *   *

They say there is no such thing as a perfect marriage, and I believe for the most part that is true. Nevertheless, I can state unequivocally that my marriage which has lasted more than thirty years has been as close to perfect as possible. This is because I have a wonderful wife. Gretchen is beautiful, sparkling with intelligence and wit, an integral part of my prosperity.

When I first met her she practically knocked my socks off. One look was all it took. What surprised me most was when I realized she would actually date me. I guess my feelings were the same as those expressed by Woody Allen in his film *Annie Hall*—the joke about how he had to be suspicious of any club that would accept him for membership. Well, that was how I felt, suspicious of any woman as perfect as Gretchen who would take me seriously enough to consider me a prospect for marriage. At twenty-two years old I didn't even take myself seriously. I was attending the University of Tennessee and knew Gretchen and Ted through a mutual friend. She always seemed out of my league but when she and Ted broke up I decided it was time to make my move. I don't know why they split, I just assumed Ted was a jerk. Anyone who would break up with Gretchen would have to be nuts, or as they say these days, cognitively challenged. But maybe she dumped him? I didn't know the details, and she wasn't about to share that information.

Ted was a sophomore then, although I never actually saw him attend class. He spent his days in the cafeteria drinking coffee and talking trash to whomever would listen. Ted liked to gossip. He also liked to share his extravagant plans. His favorite author was Ian Fleming, and like Fleming's protagonist, James Bond, Ted smoked cigarettes custom made from Turkish and Balkan Tobaccos or sometimes the dark Gauloise cigarette from France. At least that's what he told everybody. He also talked in a somewhat-less-than-convincing British accent. It was hard to imagine anyone taking Ted seriously; I didn't, but nevertheless, I sort of liked him. He was colorful, eccentric, and, if truth be known, we weren't all that dissimilar; at least at that time.

One day while I was sitting in the student food court, Ted stopped by my table. "So I hear you're going out with Gretchen now."

"That's right," I said.

"Well, I'm not going to tell you what to do. That's not my place, but I will say this: Gretchen is a whore."

"Excuse me," I said. "Please keep your opinions to yourself. I'm not interested."

"If you say so, but she'll let you do anything. That's the way she is, a real hottie, if you get my drift."

"Go away, Ted. I'm trying to study and you're annoying me."

"I should know. We went together for a long time."

"Lucky her," I said, standing up to leave. I found his behavior reprehensible. Not that I am a prude, you understand, but I can tell sour grapes from wine. Gretchen didn't deserve this—no woman did. Besides, I really liked Gretchen. In fact, I liked her so much that a month later we married.

*   *   *

After graduating, Gretchen and I moved from Tennessee. We were just starting out and we had a series of less-than-promising jobs. We moved around the country trying to find ourselves. Five years later we were settled and working back in Chattanooga. We were getting ready to take a year off to hike Europe, something we were both excited about doing. One night Ted called and told us he had married and was living in Atlanta.

"My wife and I are planning to come to Chattanooga for the weekend." He mentioned something about a spicy meeting and then asked if we could join them for dinner. He said it would be a great opportunity and I didn't know what he was talking about, but nevertheless, I agreed.

On Friday evening we met Ted and Patty at the Read House Hotel. What is it they say about beauty? It is skin deep, while ugly goes right to the bone. Patty was a singularly unattractive woman. My first impression was of a scoop of mashed potatoes flung carelessly by a cook who was five minutes past quitting time. She was massive with pasty white skin and hair the color of a rodent. Ted was her second husband which amazed me because I couldn't imagine such an unfortunate looking woman had received even one marriage proposal, much less two. She looked at least fifteen years older than Ted, and on a bad day she could have easily been mistaken for his mother. I am a little ashamed to admit that Patty's appearance brought me immense pleasure. I felt so triumphant that I didn't even mind paying for dinner. Ted had gotten what he deserved. Karma had stepped in and righted the universe.

Over dinner we heard about the three children: Amber (whom they called Amber-Darling), Phoebe, and the youngest whom they referred to as Little-Beulah. The girls were from Patty's first marriage. Between the lines, I learned Ted had gone through some disappointing jobs, and he was now working in sales for an outfit called Olympus Industries.

I kept asking myself what Ted saw in Patty. Why would he marry her? From appearances, the past few years hadn't been kind to Ted either. He was following Patty's lead toward lumpiness and no longer talking nonstop. His Bond accent was almost gone. Ted paid little attention to Gretchen and gave no hint they had previously been involved with one another. You would have thought they were meeting for the first time. Ted spoke in a slow, deliberate manner, showing little emotion. He didn't seem enthusiastic about anything except when he mentioned a sale he previously made. Then he smiled briefly. I began to suspect he might actually try to sell us something before the evening was over.

I was right. As we left the restaurant and headed toward the parking lot, Ted asked if he could "share something." Gretchen and I were anxious to make our escape, but out of politeness we followed Ted to his car. He opened his trunk and retrieved a small satchel.

Since he appeared so secretive, I thought, *Oh my God, he's selling drugs*!

But no, I couldn't have been more incorrect. Ted was trying to recruit Gretchen and me into a business enterprise where couples sell gourmet spices. It appeared to be a sort of a Ponzi scheme where one salesperson hires another "dealer," then that person, another, and so on. Each time a sale is made by someone up the chain, the first gets a percentage of commissions.

"If you have a hundred dealers working for you," Ted said. "you can make a comfortable living. And the good thing is," he continued, "you can always use the spices yourself."

Patty added, "Our girls love them. They use them on practically everything—even popcorn."

Gretchen and I listened. We thanked Ted for the opportunity to become part of the gourmet spice industry, but since we were about to leave for Europe, we explained, it wasn't a good time to launch a new career. "Maybe," I said, "when we return to the United States."

As we drove home, Gretchen and I reviewed the bizarre evening.

"What a strange fellow your old boyfriend is," I said. "I guess that's what he meant by opportunity."

"Who names a kid Amber-Darling or Little-Beulah?"

"Yeah, and what is a gourmet spice? I mean, how is it different than an ordinary spice?"

The two of us were laughing so hard I wasn't paying attention to my driving, and I guess I cut someone off because a few minutes later this car pulls along beside me with a man grimacing and extending his middle finger. I was ready to fight back and show him what a macho tough guy I was, but Gretchen was the one with sense. She reached over and prevented me from lifting my arm.

"Forget it," she said. "Ignore him. You might make things worse, and it probably was your fault, anyway. You weren't paying attention. My daddy used to say it's not a good idea to poke a sleeping bear. Daddy was a smart man."

"Okay," I said and released pressure from the accelerator.

The angry man sped away like a rocket. In a moment Gretchen and I redirected our attention again to Ted and Patty and our ridiculous evening.

*　*　*

I think it was from Paris that I had the idea to torment Ted. It was from there I sent the first postcard. I remember it had something to do with Parisian cooking, and on the picture side various spices were illustrated. I don't remember what I said, but I'm sure it was something silly, like *we are following the spice road to Istanbul. Can you use more spices?* Ted never replied.

When we returned from our year of adventure, both Gretchen and I decided to get additional education and take life more seriously. Eventually I graduated with a Master's Degree in Agricultural Engineering and Resource Management. My employment began modestly enough and not being encumbered with children we began to job-hop from one location to another. I guess that was when things started to look up.

I was on a consulting job with one of the large tropical fruit companies in Honduras when I sent Ted another postcard. Somehow I had gotten word he and Patty had divorced. I remember the postcard showed a bare-breasted, native woman with wild hair, missing teeth, and a bone through her nose. I wrote something to the effect *that if you need a new wife you might consider traveling to the Mosquito*

Coast where women are available and plenty spicy. I didn't get a reply.

After projects in Central America things began to happen fast. In addition to consulting jobs, Gretchen and I began speculating in real estate—buying and selling. We bought property in Roatan off the cost of Honduras and in Costa Rica. We flipped houses and started our own construction company. That's when we began making real money.

I'm not saying Gretchen and I got obscenely wealthy, but like the missionaries who went to Hawaii intending to do good, we did damn well. We prospered and each year our assets grew exponentially. Ten years ago we started a foundation that we named Esparanza de los Niños, which means the *hope of the children.* It's goal is to provide financial assistance to parents who were adopting internationally. We encountered so many orphans in Latin America and, being childless ourselves, we thought the foundation would be an opportunity for us to give something back.

Time sort of got away from us and the years passed

quickly. Even so, with all my projects and grueling schedule, I continued sending postcards to Ted. Sometimes I would send other things, too. One year I sent a Christmas letter. I made it look like a photocopy, the kind people receive at Christmas. It was a brag sheet of all our accomplishments during the past year. The implicit message was, weren't we something special. Look at us.

On years I wasn't bragging I sent Christmas cards, sometimes newspaper clippings. I didn't taunt him on those occasions and even wrote how much we would like to see him again. I tried to make it look sincere. Maybe he could come and visit? Of course anyone with an IQ above that of a hamster could see it was all bullshit.

I don't know why I enjoyed the thought I was bothering Ted so much. I never heard from him. Maybe he found the intrusions into his life amusing. I did. I enjoyed playing with him the way a cat enjoys tormenting a mouse. One day I googled him and nothing came up—not a word. I turned to Gretchen and said:

"It's like he never existed. Never did a damn thing—a

big zero. I wonder if he ever made a killing in the spice business? You know, I heard there was a run on marjoram."

All Gretchen said was, "Please, honey, leave him alone. You're not being nice."

*   *   *

So now we're living in Franklin, Tennessee, hobnobbing with celebrities and active in the country club scene, self-made millionaires. Gretchen is doing volunteer work. I am working hard as a philanthropist and running our foundation. I am also president of the Franklin Rotary Club. My neighbor is a state legislator and my other neighbor a country music star. My investment portfolio is impressive. In short, life is sweet.

*   *   *

I noticed the cardboard box had fallen from the man's lap and was lying on the porch. The contents lay scattered about, and I tried to make sense of what it was I was looking at. Seed packets—the kind you buy in springtime that hold vegetable or flower seeds. Then I noticed that mixed among the packages of seeds were other things, a little larger. They looked like… like postcards. Sure, that's why some had pictures while others had writing. I looked at the man's face in front of me trying to solve the puzzle. He still had a grin, but I couldn't figure why.

Then it hit me, not seeds… spices! They were cooking spices.

For a second there was a flash of recognition. It all started to come together. But it was only for the briefest of moments. I heard a noise and felt the force of something slam against my chest and knock me backward. Whatever I thought I recognized ceased to matter. I was light as a feather, as if I had no weight at all. I was either rising or the world below me was receding.

As I looked down at my property, what Gretchen and I had created, I saw the magnificence of the place in its entirety—our perfect world—a world created from our cleverness and hard work. I saw green grass, trees, and shrubbery; two lovely ponds—one with a waterfall. And for just a second I saw a koi swim by. It was lovely.

THE FAVOR*

Uncle Mike was not really Ben's uncle; he was a great uncle, the oldest brother of Ben's grandmother, Ida May, and the oldest surviving member of the family. For all of his life Ben had heard stories from his parents about Mike. Ben just called the older man Uncle Mike.

In his youth, Michael Suggs had been a robust and charismatic man. Although he now appeared frail and his stature shrunken, to Ben his uncle would forever remain the hero in the family photographs—standing tall and straight with his great mop of wavy black hair (now turned white). Ben remembered Uncle Mike as a prankster and tease with a sharp sense of humor and broad smile. With his muscular arms and chiseled face, Uncle Mike had somehow merged in Ben's mind with images of Paul Bunyan, the mythical lumberman. Ben still thought of his uncle as vibrant and larger than life, but occasionally Ben was jolted when his memories of Uncle Mike clashed with the current man who now resided in Rosewood Manor, a senior residence in Destin, Florida.

In the family photo album there was a picture of his uncle in full football uniform throwing a pass. He had been a star football player at the University of Tennessee— where he met and married a beautiful cheerleader named Patricia Grant. They fell in love and after the first date they were never apart. Against family advice, Mike and Patricia married while still in college. After graduation they both worked together as health and physical education teachers at the same high school for over thirty years. They had one child, a boy named Bruce who was killed in an automobile accident shortly after Mike and Patricia retired from school teaching. The accident had been an ominous beginning to the couple's golden years, and it was the first time Ben saw his great uncle cry. The second time Uncle Mike cried was a short time later when his beloved Patricia died from breast cancer. That was almost twenty years ago.

The town of Destin, Florida was not far from where Ben and Julie lived in the suburbs of Panama City. Once every month Ben and Julie drove to Destin to visit Uncle Mike and take him out to lunch. Afterwards Ben would call his parents in North Carolina to give a report. It was a branch of the gossip tree that helped keep the family intact.

Rosewood Manor was a plush complex with three dining rooms, a library, swimming pool, and a theater on the premises. Ben hoped he and Julie could live as comfortably when they were old. Best of all for Uncle Mike, the complex was located adjacent to a public golf course.

Until recently Uncle Mike played eighteen holes a day—without a cart. Now at his advanced age, he was still a striking figure with a shock of white hair and bushy white eyebrows, cracking jokes and flashing his youthful smile. His favorite line was that the Florida heat made him randy and caused his memory to fail. He kept pretending to forget the name of his companion, Madge, whom he met two years ago. She was a widow and enjoyed pampering Uncle Mike. Madge also lived at Rosewood Manor, which the two referred to as God's waiting room. Uncle Mike joked that he and his "girlfriend" planned to take up surfboarding. "We're waiting to catch the perfect wave," he would say, winking at Madge. "While we're waiting for our number to be called, we might as well be surfing." Then in a burst of enthusiasm he'd clap his hands together, "Get your bathing suit honey, surf's up."

In October Uncle Mike had been diagnosed with prostate cancer, and in November he had begun treatment. Ben's parents had visited for the holidays, and it was a somber Christmas. Since then, Ben and Julie watched as Uncle Mike lost the energy and vitality that had so much defined him. Ben wasn't sure if the dramatic decline was due to the treatment or the cancer itself, but did it matter? Either way Ben feared the worse—Uncle Mike was very old, and Ben was a realist.

Three weeks ago at their last visit, Ben had been discouraged by what he saw. Uncle Mike was beyond thin; he was a ghost of his former self. His face seemed haunted by large, dark eyes, and he was too weak to stand when Ben and Julie entered the room. No lunch was served that day. Madge sat quietly by his side, patiently attending to his needs. A type of telepathy had developed between Uncle Mike and

Madge. He need only to look or flick his fingers in a certain direction and Madge would know exactly what he meant.

On Saturday morning Ben and Julie drove to Rosewood Manor. It was eleven o'clock when they knocked on the cheerful yellow door. Madge greeted them warmly and they followed her inside. The living room was now functioning as a bedroom, with a bed positioned by the sliding glass patio doors.

"It's easier this way," Madge explained. "He likes to watch the big TV and now he can see the squirrels on the patio. He enjoys animals. Yesterday he saw a lizard."

Madge pointed to the dining table positioned at the foot of Uncle Mike's bed. One corner of the table was covered with containers of pills and medical supplies, along with an impressive stack of papers that looked to be receipts and medical forms. Madge had cleared a space on the table and set out coffee cups and cookies. After greeting Uncle Mike, Ben and Julie settled into their seats. Madge poured coffee and quietly took her own seat at Uncle Mike's bedside.

The back of the bed was raised so Uncle Mike was

in a sitting position with his legs stretched out before him. Under the white sheet Ben saw the outline of a body so thin and small it looked like a child's. Madge must have seen the concern on Ben's face. "Your uncle's a little tired today," she said. "Last night was difficult. He couldn't keep his food down."

Uncle Mike sank comfortably into his pillows and smiled.

"I'm fine," he said. "How're your folks, Ben?"

As they talked, Ben relaxed. He was relieved to notice that his uncle remained upbeat. Uncle Mike might be weak, but he was not defeated. This was a positive piece of information Ben could share with his parents. After the initial pleasantries, his uncle turned to him and said, "I want to thank you for coming; the two of you."

Ben protested, "No....no. There's no need to thank us. We enjoy visiting"

Uncle Mike slowly shook his head. "... Well, I didn't just call for a visit. This is more than a visit." With that he turned toward Madge and raised his right hand slightly, pointing toward the patio.

Madge continued on Uncle Mike's behalf. "Your uncle needs to ask you a favor, Ben. But first, can you please bring something in from the patio? It's just inside the storage room, behind the door on the left…there's a burlap sack on the floor. Could you get that for your uncle, please?"

"Sure," Ben replied, surprised. He left the table and walked out through the sliding glass doors to the patio with Julie behind him. In the storage room, just as Madge had said, he found the burlap sack, and lifted it. "Holy Mackerel," Ben exclaimed. "This is heavy. It feels like there's a rock in here." He hauled the bag back into the living room and plopped it down on the floor beside the bed where his uncle could see it by leaning to one side.

"Now open it please, so you can see what's inside."

Ben untied the bag, and pulled the sides down, revealing a large slab of gray stone. Ben stared a moment, perplexed.

It was Julie who responded first. "Is it a gravestone?" She asked

Ben looked up at Uncle Mike, wondering what was going on. "Is it a gravestone?" he repeated. "You have a gravestone?"

Uncle Mike was lying perfectly still with his eyes closed. "Yes," he sighed, sounding tired and distant. "I have a gravestone. I've been toting it around more than seventy years—hard to believe."

Speechless, Ben and Julie examined the headstone. It appeared old and worn. It was almost two feet high, with an irregular bottom where it had been broken off at its base. It was several inches thick, and the figure of a lamb had been carved, resting on top of the stone. The carving was quite intricate and the lamb appeared peaceful. Beneath the lamb on the face of the stone were engraved the words: Sarah Burns. Beloved Daughter. Our Precious Lamb. 1879 - 1890.

"Who is Sarah Burns?" Ben asked.

Uncle Mike inhaled deeply, his eyes still closed. There was a long pause. Then he opened his eyes and said softly: "I need to explain. When I was a boy my family moved around the country. My dad was a salesman and the company he worked for was always changing his territory. For a while we lived in the Midwest....all over, really. When I was fifteen, we lived in Michigan, smack dab in the middle of the mitten. One night I was out with a couple of buddies, riding around in a friend's pickup truck. One of the guys was older and could drive. Anyway, our school football team had just won a big game and we were celebrating. It was more than just a game really, it was the state championship. It was a really big deal. I remember we played Niles High School that night. Sometimes it seems just like yesterday. Our team was undefeated that year.

"Well, there were three of us and we had been drinking beer. We were just driving around the countryside when we came to a church in the middle of nowhere. We stopped the truck because one of the guys was going to be sick and we didn't want him to puke in the truck. At the side of the church there was a cemetery. We started walking around the cemetery and began to horse-around. Then this guy—Tom was his name—he picked up a piece of wood...a stick...

that was lying on the ground. It was a tree branch. A big one. He swung it like a baseball bat and he hit a headstone. The headstone fell over and we all started laughing. Next thing you know, we're taking turns swinging the branch and hitting gravestones. Some fell over, most didn't. When it was my turn I went to this headstone and gave it a mighty whack. The stone cracked towards the bottom and fell over. It only took one hit. Broke the branch too. It was then I noticed the carving. I couldn't see very clearly because it was dark, with only the truck headlights. But in the light it looked special to me. So I, in all the wisdom of fifteen years and also being intoxicated, decided it would make a good souvenir. I picked it up and put it in the back of the truck."

Uncle Mike paused for several seconds. "I never felt good about what I did that night. Almost immediately I regretted it… felt guilty. The next morning I was ashamed of myself. I didn't want my parents to know, so I hid the stone in some bushes behind the garage where my parents wouldn't find it. I really intended to return it someday, but I never did. My friend with the truck got in trouble and was grounded, and I couldn't drive. I was too cowardly to tell my parents what had happened. So, to make a long story short, I put the whole thing in the back of my mind. But I couldn't forget about it completely, and each time I moved, I brought the headstone along. I don't know how I kept it a secret for so long. After I got married I told Patricia about it and showed her the stone."

Uncle Mike paused and smiled. "Your Aunt Patricia had a fit—she wouldn't let me keep it in the house…put it in the garden instead. After Bruce died she said I should take it back where it belonged. Pat's thinking changed a lot after Bruce passed; I guess mine did too. Pat believed Sarah would never rest in peace as long as her grave marker was missing. She thought Sarah's ghost would torment me. I told her there are no such things as ghosts. We planned to take it back, together, but we never did. I never did. One thing leads to another. Then Pat got sick. It always just seemed to get put off. I let her down, and Bruce, too." Tears began to form and Uncle Mike's voice grew unsteady. "Now I can't take it back. Look at me. It's too late." He paused to catch his breath.

"Uncle Mike, you're getting too upset," Ben said. "You needn't worry so much over this. It was a long time ago, and there was no real harm done, was there? You made a mistake, that's all. You were just a kid. It was a simple mistake that no one will hold against you."

But his uncle seemed not to hear. "I think the little town was Wind? It was first named Dutchville in the 1800's. My dad told me that. He said it was also called Hardscrabble, too, because there were so many stones in the ground. It must have been hard to farm the soil. I don't know if they had tractors back then....must have farmed with horses. I don't know. Even with a tractor it would be hard to farm land so full of rocks. I don't know why a town would have so many names. Maybe they called it Dutchville because they had a lot of Dutch people living there. Do you think that could be why?"

"Uncle Mike," Ben replied: "You're drifting. It doesn't matter what the town was called, or the technology of agriculture they used back then. It was a long time ago."

Julie leaned over the stone and touched it. With her fingertips she traced over the lamb, as if petting it. Uncle Mike watched and continued, "It was just a short way from Mt. Pleasant, the town where we lived....in 1932, the year of the championship game. But I'm not sure." He looked at Ben, with pleading eyes. "That's the whole point. I'm not sure what the town was called. I can't remember."

Uncle Mike wiped tears from his eyes and sobbed. "I wish I had never done that terrible thing. I don't even know if the town still exists. It could be a ghost town. There may be nothing..."

"Please," Ben pleaded, griping his uncle's hand. "This isn't good for you. You're too upset."

"If you could just help me," his uncle pleaded. "You're the only one I know who can help."

"How?" Ben asked. "What can I do?"

"Promise me you'll find that church and return the headstone."

"What?" Ben was flabbergasted. He looked to Julie for support, but she seemed equally surprised. She quickly removed her hands from the stone and sat upright next to her husband.

"Uncle Mike. Do you realize what you're asking? You said yourself you don't know where that church is! Maybe it isn't even there anymore. It's been over seventy years. How would I ever find it?"

"Ben, you are a clever boy and you have a smart wife—smart and pretty." There was a flicker of the old Mike in his eye, but only for a moment. "One place is like another. These days all places look the same even though they are different. There is the interstate and maps. You have heard of a road atlas. There are even global positioning devices available. I read about them in my AARP magazine. You could make an adventure out of it. Go on an action vacation and have fun. Michigan is a nice place to visit. You could see Detroit."

"Detroit? Why would I want to see Detroit? Do you know what the crime rate is in Detroit? I don't want to get mugged."

"I think of you as a son, Ben, and I'm leaving most of

what I have to you and Julie—except for what I set aside for my sweetie. There will be plenty left for you to pay for this project."

"You know money's not the point," Ben replied.

"So will you do it?"

"I'll think about it, okay? I don't know if I can do it."

"That's not good enough. I need a promise. After I'm gone you will return the headstone. And when you get to Michigan I want you to tell Sarah how very sorry I am for what I did." Uncle Mike looked like he might cry again. "Ask her to forgive me. I keep thinking that marker could have been on Brucie's grave. What could I have been thinking?"

"Okay, Uncle Mike, I can promise this: I'll do my best—I promise. Now, can we talk about this later when you're feeling better?"

"You promise, Ben?"

"I promise."

"Take it with you today, okay? Please? I've kept it long enough—a life time. Will you take it home with you?"

"Alright," Ben agreed. "If it makes you feel better, I'll take it."

"Thank you," Uncle Mike sighed in relief. He seemed to deflate like a balloon. "I know it's a lot to ask. I want you both to know how much I appreciate this. It's very important to me."

"Yes," Julie answered, "we can see that. Now please don't worry about it any more."

The remainder of the visit was short. When they left, Ben took the bag with Sarah's headstone and put it in the trunk of the car.

As they drove home Julie asked: "Are you really going to return that thing?"

"I don't know," Ben said. "Maybe... we'll see. Uncle Mike will get well soon and the whole thing will probably be forgotten. Maybe this episode was just a reaction to his medications or treatment."

"I hope so, but I'm not so sure. It felt funny touching that stone. I had a strange sensation."

"What do you mean? What kind of sensation?"

"I'm not sure," Julie replied. "Emptiness... loneliness... like something wasn't right."

"You're being dramatic. You're too sensitive. This isn't a movie, Julie; just an unusual request from a very sick old man."

"But maybe it is like a movie, Ben, and now we're part of it."

"I don't know what you're talking about," Ben replied. "The only sensation I had was that the stone was heavy. And then, too, there was the sense of obligation. That's was even heavier and it's a feeling I don't like."

"You may not like it, Ben, but you will do it. You will take this gravestone for Uncle Mike and you will drive it to a place where you have never been. Even though the request is heavy and will require real effort, you will do it. You will do it because you are a good man who keeps his word, and that's one of the reasons why I married you. So maybe we should go home and pack."

BOOKS BY JIM & CHERYL PAHZ

McAngel

Ben and Julie Pearson have an uncle who is dying of cancer. One day the uncle makes an unusual request. He wants them to go to Michigan on his behalf and return a broken cemetery headstone. He stole the stone when he was a teenager and now he is overcome with remorse. Ben and Julie promise to return the headstone, and are faced with the challenge of keeping their word. They receive advice from Billy, a disabled man they meet at McDonalds. Billy appears unkempt, speaks in riddles, and claims to be an angel. But the young couple is skeptical. What kind of angel hangs out at McDonalds and has crumbs in his beard? Do angels really exist ... and if they do would you recognize one if he stood in front of you? These are the questions Ben and Julie ask as they embark on the adventure of their lives.

Almost Chosen... Nearly Saved

With a Jewish father and a Baptist mother, Daniel Fisher grows into a confused and alienated young man, uncertain of his place in the world. His search for identity takes him from the bible belt of the south to the Negev Desert of Israel. Along the way he stumbles into love with Mia Murphy, a fellow seeker and soul mate. To obtain the missing piece that will complete their lives, Daniel and Mia must travel to a tiny village in the jungle of Guatemala. Their search ends when they find an orphaned baby who needs them as much as they need her. They name the child Quetzal, after the beautiful bird that is the symbol of Guatemala. The quetzal bird is unable to survive captivity. It lives hidden from man in the cloud forests of Guatemala and Costa Rica. In this novel, this majestic bird symbolizes the meaning and purpose that Daniel Fisher is seeking. The quetzal is also a metaphor for the futility of those who claim ownership of God. Like the quetzal, God cannot be confined to any one religion.

Quetzal

When Quetzal Maya Fisher decides to uncover the mystery of her past and heritage, she begins at the place where she was placed for adoption, the Evangelical Friendship Mission of Guatemala. A mother herself, Quetzal visits Guatemala to learn about Felicita, the birthmother who released her as a baby for adoption. Quetzal uncovers secrets about Tommy Tuttle and his wife, Grace, who ran the mission, and she learns about the adoption scandal that nearly brought them down. The history of the mission and the players involved are told through the eyes of Quetzal and follows the threads of her life to discover her past and find her future. Along the way she learns about love, sacrifice, and the true meaning of family.

About the Author

Since encountering his first bull,
Jim Pahz has liked to tell stories.
Currently, Jim lives in Central
Michigan with his wife Cheryl.
Together they have written three
novels, *McAngel, Almost Chosen...
Nearly Saved,* and *Quetzal.*

Please visit them at their website:
www.pahz.net